You will... questions...
Best wishes
from Richard xxx

GW00393859

The Writer's Bin

By
Richard J Small

Exploring the bin contents of an English author and more than 60 short stories and poems of varying genres, adventure, philosophical, cautionary, sad, thought provoking, humorous and some simply born of madness.

**Dedicated to all free minded people,
whoever and wherever they may be.**

My thanks to John and Elizabeth Dawson
for all their help with editing.

Other books by the same author

I want to tell you a story
   Edward Gaskell Publishers

Ghosts and Things
   Edward Gaskell Publishers

Tales from Merlin's Pal
   Edward Gaskell Publishers

Simple Poems
   Edward Gaskell Publishers

Tai Chi and Aikido –
exploring pathways beyond choreography
   Goodnessmepublishing.co.uk

My Devon tales
   Goodnessmepublishing.co.uk

Contents

My friend's dog
Elsa exploring Cornwall

'It can't be that bad!'

'Hey, what's up? Nothing can be that bad.'

'I've lost something, something I didn't realise was so precious to me.'

'Not to worry, I'll help you find it.'

'It's no good, nobody can help. If only I'd been more careful.'

'Hey, look, nothing is worth making all this fuss, if it was that important, get another one.'

'Afraid I can't, unique - Only ever one of them. If only I hadn't wasted it.'

'Well let's backtrack a bit, see if we can find where you lost it. What say you?'

'I think it was lost a long time ago but I only just felt its loss now, only now.'

'Well, if you lost it a long time ago without even noticing, it couldn't have been that important, could it?'

'Oh, yes, it was, I should have treasured it more. Made the most of it and now it is too late. No matter how I try, I can never get it back.'

'Obviously you won't let me help you, so, what was it you lost?'

'My youth.'

Beginning of the end

Life's not over, not quite yet,
no guarantee, not worth a bet.
I try to keep myself from harm,
out of reach, of death's long arm.

At our club there once were five,
'none of us can leave, alive.'
The man that said this, our friend Joe,
sad to say, the first to go.

Four remain, to keep the faith,
dodging devils and the wraith.
Armed and trained in martial skill,
we yet defy, the reaper's will.

Something says, the time draws near,
but, funny thing, I have no fear.
Too late to right those life's wrongs now,
we know it ends – but just not how.

Some find in this, a touch of shame,
and others still, will lay the blame.
Regardless of, how 'tis I fall,
know this my friends, God bless you all.

Guest Adviser.

The Official review site that balances trip adviser, serving all associated Hotels, Inns and B&Bs.

Reviews.
* Excellent   (1)
* Good   (3)
* Avoid if possible   (25)
* Place on 'no vacancies' list (47)
* Not even house trained   (18)

Search by name   ………………
Include pseudonyms or alias   ……………..…

Name.   Address.   Facebook.   Twitter.   E mail addresses.   Other social media.
…………….   ………………   ……………   ………….
………………..   ………………
Examples below:-

Ms Marjorie Poopzucker   Eagles Nest Allhallows Lane, Bristol. Known on social media as Cleopatra53

Asked for early breakfast, arrived late, demanded two fried eggs but only ate the yokes. Spilled coffee over table cloth while shaking the last drops out of café tier.
Never thoughtful, polite or respectful.
Complained about a droning noise from the Inn and which kept her awake all night – room service staff traced the noise to her mobile phone set on vibrate – 48 missed facebook messages.

Mr Robert Sly   4 Smithfield Gardens, Oxmoor (Council Estate) Known on social media as 'the proffesser'!

In more senses of the word as you can imagine, he is an **amateur** biologist specialising in parasites.

Founder of the organisation, 'Tics need friends too'.

Spent his daylight hours collecting tics from moorland bracken, dying sheep and any dog that came in the bar. Turned his guest room into a makeshift laboratory (read menagerie). After a couple of subsequent guests went down with Lyme's disease we had the first floor fumigated and deep cleaned. Cost ran to nearly £3000, including lost bookings.

Mr William Choker.   Flat 22 Marx House (Social housing unit) next to Parkhust Hospital

Known on social media as, 'the quackbuster'.

Despite clearly being advised several times that our Inn is pet friendly, Mr Choker insisted upon booking a room – our best room – and for one week.

The man is rabidly allergic to dogs and threw up on a number of occasions, twice in the dining room at busy mealtimes and once over a visiting walker's Rottweiler. Mr Choker skilfully avoided throwing up in the same place twice, each time he managed to find somewhere new.

Mr Choker demanded a full refund on all meals as he claimed he had 'Not had them long enough to do him any good.'

Our cleaning bill ran into hundreds of pounds.

Apparently, the walker can no longer persuade his Rottweiler to enter another pub, despite being regularly medicated with tranquilisers.

Earl of Widdleport, the right honourable Lord Peregrine Slavering-Smythe

Unknown address. No social Media content.

NB Couldn't spell properly when filling in registration form and tried to pay with a Social Services food voucher. Only booked our cheapest room.

Claims he lost our towels on a picnic at the beach and the tide took them out. Meanwhile he used our velvet curtains on which to wipe his hands, nose and anything else he felt required attention.

Despite the best efforts of our staff, he managed to con several other guests into buying him beer and food with the promise of an invitation to the House of Lords or a trip on his yacht to the Maldives.

A total charlatan and most unpleasant character. It was obvious that he preferred to urinate in the sink, which was closer to his bed by a yard than the toilet. When he left without paying, he took with him all of the toiletries, including the loo roll and no doubt a few souvenirs from the bar, the loss of which we have yet to discover.

A word to the wise – the ability of a guest to spell or use grammar correctly is inversely proportional to the likelihood they will complain about you on Trip Adviser.

St Crispin's Twins

The new twins were a most welcome addition to the household. The fact that they were brown in a predominantly white neighbourhood didn't matter; no one ever commented, not once. Their first forays into the wide wild world were taken with great care. They were so tense when young and almost certainly over protected. As time wore on, so did they and age took its toll. Once, in an unguarded moment one of the twins was brutally savaged by a family dog, leaving a permanent disfigurement and a reluctance to be seen in public. However, the other sibling dug his heels in and made him toe the line, made him walk again, even into the crowded town. The more they went out, the more relaxed they became, almost uncaring about what should befall them next. Before they became too old for it, they were adventurers, of raging rivers, moors, and mountains, nothing stood in their way. Once they both had a go at fire walking. They would tell you, it's not true you don't get at least a bit singed! I suppose by then, they had nothing much left to lose.

I still have treasured photographs and I remember them with great affection. They were born together and they died together, never having been parted in all their lives. Somewhere out there, they will both be resolutely trudging some time-worn esoteric path. Perhaps you will meet them one day – if so, please say hello, and tell them, I remember.

Ah, Boretum.

It was budget day in July of 2015.

"Oh will oh will they taxus, Baccata?" asked Hazel, though she couldn't stop too long as her horse 'Chestnut', was tethered to a kiddie's maple outside and would pine for her return.

"Ashually, we can holda them at a bay if we just get sycamore and claima da big benefits," slurred the sloshed Portuguese poet laureliate, Elmo Baccatta.

"That's oakay for yew to say," replied hazel who was of good heart even if her friend Ivy, the clingy old parasite, wood sap her strength somewhat. Hazel decided to spruce herself up then conifer with the copse before daring to branch out and break the law.

The copse were indeed helpful and all three of them, Inspector Larch, Sergeant Wal Nut the elder and PC Rowan Berry all twigged her dilemma straight away, "Yew and I can cedar problem here Hazel but it's holly unlikely that Elmo will get away with such deceit, mind you, he is much alder than us."

"He'll be getting the birch if he carries on like this, you make a right pear you do and he'll drop you plum in it if you're not careful."

"You won't be poplar but you'll have to change his mind"

"The home office already badly want to prunus," said the tree copse in unison.

Hazel nodded, fir a moment she considered that a holiday might help Elmo, perhaps Cypress would be nice at this time of year.

Riding home on sweet chestnut she stopped off at hawthorns confectioners, as they might have some plane chocolate for a treat.

Now I may be barking up the wrong tree, but I guess you are busy wondering if I've missed any. I may well have beech you to it !

Cherry ho for now,

Oliver Mimosa and Tamerisk Sumach, xx

In order of appearance;-

Arboretum, Willow, Taxus Baccata, Hazel, Horse Chestnut, Maple, Pine, Ash, Bay, Portuguese Laurel, Elm, Oak, Yew, heart, Ivy, wood, sap, Spruce, Conifer, copse, branch, Larch, Walnut, Elder, Rowan, twig, Cedar, Holly, Alder, Birch, Pear, Plum, Poplar, Prunus, tree, Fir, Cypress, Sweet Chestnut, Hawthorn, Plane, bark, Beech, Cherry, Olive, Mimosa, Tamerisk, Sumach.

Animal Idioms

Well, there he was, stubborn as a donkey, huffin and puffin, ferreting around in the kitchen drawer.

'Hold your horses,' I said, 'you're like a pig headed bull in a china shop. Come on,' I said, 'let the dog see the rabbit.'

Of course it was too late, with all his monkeying around, the horse had bolted and what he was looking for was lost. I suppose leopards don't change their spots, he'll always have the memory of an elephant with amnesia. When he saw I was angry his mood went through scaredy cat to possum.

'You can forget those crocodile tears,' I told him. And after all that, he'd been on a wild goose chase and opened a can of worms for nothing – it wasn't even in the kitchen drawer – it was in his pocket all the time.

Teenagers eh?

Animal liberation -
and the price to be paid.

They seemed like a normal family, but they shared a dangerous secret. The father, who we will call Teddy, while working a day job in a local high street shop, was also a clandestine member of the banned organisation, the Animal Liberation Army, (ALA). Teddy had already survived one arrest, the police not finding enough evidence to make bring charges. Teddy was vehemently opposed to any animal rights abuse and was often out casing factories and farms, just a man out walking his dog.

They functioned much like a terrorist cell, never using real names or meeting in public. They operated out of an internet cafe to avoid being traced. Theirs was a small group of five, code name 'the free bears'. We will only mention one other of them by name and that is Barney.

Barney was a strange man in his mid-thirties, reclusive, and living alone with a barn owl he had single handed rescued from its nest, he was a fanatic. Barney never made his views public. Without attention drawn to him, he could liberate far more birds and animals than was possible by lawful means. Though he would tell you his cause was legitimate, morally if not by statute. The thought of factory farmed chickens sickened him, as did all forms of animal captivity if the truth were known. Oddly though, he thought it was okay to breed mice for the owl. After all, that was simply nature operating as she should. There was a bonus for the local wild bird population too, which unexpectedly flourished in his neighbourhood after several of the local cats went walkabout. Fortunately, their owners were never to witness the tabby coloured owl pellets regurgitated by Barney's pet.

Whatever you think of such activities, be it by the liberationists or the farmers, Teddy and Barney were devout believers in their cause. Followers of a noble purpose, humane and sympathetic, they were a secret society of vegetarian freedom fighters and, heroes all.

Okay, so one or two things hadn't worked out so well, like the hundreds of mink rescued from becoming fur coats and released into the wild to wreak havoc on indigenous wildlife and domestic animals alike. Tough, vicious, with voracious appetites, they spread like wildfire, decimating populations as they went. They are still out there. The wild boar release went better and if nothing else would stop people poking about in the forests for fear of meeting and upsetting one. Thirty thousand pheasants were rescued in a single night, birds that were destined to be at least shot at, if not shot itself. That is, if the beaters could get the well-fed tame birds into the air. The ensuing extensive damage to growing crops by thousands of hungry pheasants was a sacrifice all vegetarians must put up with if their beliefs are genuine enough.

Now Teddy's group had a plan, a big plan. One that would make them as famous as Disney World, The Klu Klux Klan or the Nazi Party. They planned to liberate the entire population of a provincial zoo.

Each member of the team took B&B or camping accommodation in separate locations along the Devon coast. They would only meet at the appointed hour near the zoo on the moor before moving in for the kill. Operation *'serves 'em right'* was underway. Although dawn broke early at that time of year, the staff didn't arrive to open the cages and feed the residents until seven thirty.

Dorothy was a young graduate in her early thirties and loved the animals. She had brought the zoo's young leopard up from a cub and had a strong bond with the now fully grown cat. Dorothy's first indication that something awful had happened was when she saw a dead giraffe by a roadside cottage, she later discovered that it had been electrocuted when it walked into the cottage overhead power cables.

The zoo was only a few hundred yards further on, so she delayed telephoning for help until she arrived at the open gates. There were gates and fences down all over the place, but a few animals had remained, feeling safer in their homes than out there in the unknown. The remainder of the now fully alerted staff arrived and Bob Shepherd the senior supervisor and qualified vet, split the staff into teams of two with strict instructions to search the area with great caution. Mr Shepherd handed out tranquiliser guns from the boot of his car.

Dorothy passed under the great oak tree, oblivious that the leopard was up there with a convenient meal that he'd secured without effort once the saboteurs had opened the gates. The leopard watched with typical cat-like interest and a full tummy. He was sharing a branch quite amicably with an eagle owl that was busy plucking what had once been a rare and endangered Burmese wild fowl. Two of those predictions had now proved to be true, it was wild, and it was certainly endangered now, in fact it was beyond both those stages. Higher up, an alpha male baboon was still thoughtfully playing with the dead body of a rare lesser spotted lemur that foolishly had also explored the same tree in search of liberation. The baboon had cheerfully helped the process by liberating the lemur's soul from its body. As they carefully searched the premises, temporarily repairing fences and gates as they went, it became more apparent what had transpired.

The Iguanas had enjoyed a feast in the butterfly house almost as much as the mink had, in the Koi pond. The wolves were some thirty miles away having run a prize red deer stag to ground, they too had full tummies and lay contented in the bracken enjoying a well-earned rest in the sun.

The phone rang, it was local farmer who wanted someone to collect a zebra that had become rather too fond of one of his donkeys. The meerkats were still sound asleep in their burrows, they knew when it wasn't breakfast time.

Upon entering the reptile house, they were in for a shock. In front of an empty aquarium, which bore a small label, 'Spitting Cobra, Africa', lay the body of a man. His face obviously contorted in pain despite the balaclava. Teddy's lifeless and blood shot eyes stared at them in silent disbelief. The cobra would have seen those eyes too, just as the lid to home was removed. No second invitation required, the great eyeballs in the sky breaking into his home were dealt with swiftly.

Quite a few animals were returning to their enclosures after a brief dally with freedom, after all, it was close to feeding time and they knew where free meals were served. For a reason other than becoming prey, being run over or electrocuted, the big black cat never did return. He was off to the moors to find his relatives – he'd heard a lot about them from visitors to his enclosure. Now was his chance to meet the family.

Dorothy walked back to the main gate. As she walked under the great oak, she heard a growl and looked up. She was as excited to see the leopard as he was to see her. Grabbing his kill to share with Dorothy, the leopard was soon on the ground. He dropped the half eaten and disembowelled gift at Dorothy's feet and pressed his head against her legs, purring like an old tabby just let in from the cold. As Dorothy reached down by habit to scratch the big cat's ears she convulsed with nausea as Barney's terrified but lifeless eyes looked their last upon the sky.

Barney and Teddy might not have bought a ticket for the zoo but had paid their entrance fee to the next world, having been themselves liberated from all earthly concerns. Dorothy pulled the leopard away from finishing his meal before the police arrived and the zoo reopened the following month, the publicity having worked magic for the bank balance. People queued for hours to take selfies by the plaque under the oak tree.

'Barney the bungling burglar died here,
killed by unknown liberated animal.'

'mmm, they look tasty.'

Not my funeral - but it could be yours.

A rainbow coloured, state of the art, funeral limousine stopped quietly outside, its EU badge of 48 stars surrounding a picture of a crematorium prominent on the bonnet. A young woman in an attractive short blue Ibiza style party dress alighted and with laptop in hand she approached the door.

'Bing Bong,' went the doorbell. Eventually the door was opened by an old man wearing comfortable 'sit about the house watching daytime TV' clothes. He peered into the light of day, 'Yes dear? Can I help you?'

'Oh, hello, I'm sorry about your sad news and we've come to pick up the dead body for the funeral. As you know,' she continued in a truly delightful eastern European accent, 'The EU department for standardised burials, cremations and pension reduction initiatives, arranges everything. The mourners were all contacted by facebook or twitter and are waiting in the obligatory electric cars outside.'

'What's that to do with me?' asked the old fellow, fumbling for his glasses so he could have a better look at that party dress.

Ladvia, funeral representative and pension reduction technician, having inherited all the instincts and skills of her KGB grandfather, looked at her notes. 'You are Mr John Smith age 83 of 3 Botfly Avenue, New Hamburg, are you not?'

The old chap was getting some of his marbles together now and was used to dealing with cold callers, who incidentally were usually from the French Farmer's Benefits Association. That is, ever since double glazing and religious callers were banned by the EU Cult and Insurgency Eradication Programme. As a former trade union shop steward, he knew a thing or two about negotiating from strength.

'Well bits of that are correct, you've done well with the address dear, and the name is nearly right. You're ten years out with the age, I'm 93 and my name is Jim, Jim Smith. The other bit that you seem to have mistaken, is that I'm not actually dead yet.'

'Oh, dear, are you sure? It says here... look.... quite clearly, we are to pick up a body for immediate processing and despatch. All the documents are signed by the Strasburg Intelligence Unit, the crematorium fees have already been paid, interment documents completed, the mourners informed and ordered to attend and I'm afraid your old UK pension has been terminated and funds transferred to the Commission for Redistribution. There's nothing I can do; the EU will not compromise or renegotiate on this.'

'Be that as it may Miss, but I'm not dead and, old as I am, I will resist your offer of incineration with every sinew of my body. I'm stronger than I look you know.' Jim said defiantly as he leaned on the front door frame of his dilapidated one-bedroom council bungalow for support.

Ladvia realised there was indeed a mistake, a computer glitch no doubt, as ever since artificial intelligence was given the authority to run the department several similar errors had occurred. Luckily some of the elderly people died of shock when the authorities called for their bodies and the self-fulfilling edict ensured that the funerals went ahead as planned. This Jim or John bloke looked like he might have a few years left in him - but not if she could help it. Rules are rules, (except in France where they had arranged a separate treaty to break them as necessary in return for handing over parts of Cornwall to Germany).

'Why don't we find you some nice clothes and take you for a ride in our delightful car. . . you can sit in the front with me.' Ladvia smiled a charming smile, the sort that Jim had only ever seen on the big screen, back when his eyesight was still functioning normally. However, he had a mind to go along with the invitation and nodded to Ladvia to enter. Jim enjoyed Ladvia's charming company as she rooted through his wardrobe looking for something suitable to be buried in. A quick wash and brush up and a loosely fitting old suit hanging on his shoulders and which he'd last worn some 40 years previous - when he was a few stone heavier. Now he looked the part of the requisite internment candidate.

Of course, none of the incumbent mourners recognised him or remembered what he looked like in order to confirm he was indeed the deceased because he'd moved to the South West over 50 years ago and had changed quite a bit. One of the mourners commented, 'My god, he's shrunk a lot, he was a six footer when I knew him and look, he's grown hair . . . he was bald as a badger when I worked with him at the horse and donkey abattoir.'

Ladvia, like her Russian grandfather, didn't want to fail at the first hurdle, so Jim, coming along for the ride, would appease the throng of mourners who had travelled from as far as Australia to see him buried and hear the reading of his apparently substantial will. Rumour had it that he was worth millions and known to be generous. For many this was a funeral to die for. You don't get many invites to funerals like this.

It's a long time since Jim had been out in a car ... a posh one like that anyway. She helped him into the front seat and gauged his health, there was still a chance if they play their cards right, they might be able to bury this chap anyway. ... whoever he was... at least the mourners can go home happy and the funeral directors have already paid the cremation fees by a deduction through the pension levy.

Ladvia tried everything she knew. She had the driver put the climate control on freeze and stopped off for a double cheeseburger and chips with chilli sauce for the intended deceased. She even resorted to fondling his knee, hoping for a heart attack. The trouble is, Jim was having the time of his life and thought happily to himself as he wiped his sweating brow with a cheap serviette, 'I really must get out more.'

Three times the driver had to drive by the crematorium, each time to a flurry of activity by the waiting Crematorium Executive Operatives First Class, all on EU minimum wage of 4 Euros an hour, and to the frustrated excitement of the following mourners. Three times they drove around the town, each time worse than the next for old Mr Corbun, who was feeling rather travel sick. He was travelling alone and had no family, in fact some of the other mourners had a suspicion he was a professional wake crasher and only in it for the free sandwiches.

Ladvia's earpiece crackled subversively into life. It was wonderful news and couldn't have come at a better time. It was Ahmed the Turkish driver of mourner's transport car three. 'Ms Ladvia, we have a body, Mr Corbun has choked on his vomit and none of the other passengers are willing to give mouth to mouth. Of course, I would, but section D of paragraph 2, part 1b of the EU burial operative's regulations forbids a driver to leave the controls of his vehicle while still in motion.'

Ladvia smiled a smile of contentment as she revelled in completion of another demographical statistic and took her hand off Jim's sweaty knee.

'He can catch the bus home,' she thought.

The EU will have their funeral after all.

***

Amber eyes, amber warning.

This is my version of an extract from another author's story about an abandoned building with surprisingly not a sign of vandalism.

With fallen rose petals underfoot, she had peered in wonder through the old dark glass. Past her own reflection, she peered at another time, another world. It was a world to which she felt a strange belonging.

She could be the girl she could see by the mirror, in the chair, with dog at feet, comfortable near the warmth of the cooking range, secure in a home that afforded velvet curtains, happy in her world of daydreams.

A toad with amber eyes moved at her feet and in her looking, she found the alluring rusty key.

She felt like she belonged beyond that windowpane and, key in hand, she entered. She stepped in quickly, eager to relive her vision through the window's mind. Only a few steps in, her nostrils filled with that dank stagnant smell that always lives on in abandoned buildings when everything else is dead.

Her feet felt the long lived icy cold of the flagstones and her heart shuddered within her body, as disappointment met cold in the middle. She turned to leave quickly, just as the door was slowly creaking closed – it was only a few steps to the door but cobwebs clawed at her face as if to keep her there, keep her now, where she didn't want to stay.

'What a mistake, you silly girl,' she told herself as she hurriedly escaped and locked the door behind her.

Replacing the key exactly where she'd found it, she became aware of looking into the amber eyes of the toad. She sensed the toad was sharing some wisdom with her, she opened her mind to listen. . .

'Looking through the glass will never tell you what is on the other side, looking with imagination belies the reality of a different existence. Outside the glass you were anyone you wished to be – inside, something sought to rob you of your soul.

In life, you will find many windows through which you may be encouraged to look – remember well – 'seeing is never seeing.'

She'd found more in a moment from the amber eyes than the old house could tell in a lifetime, who's ever lifetime it was!

Sadly, she didn't listen, and Alice would go on to make a crazy mistake once more.

***

Beware the dancing weasel.
A short tale of caution from the U.S.A

Little Daniel Bronson was one of four children, all boys. His parents were quite poor but none the less always gave their sons as a good a holiday each year as they could afford. It became obvious during these holidays how different Daniel was to the others. His siblings, Donald, Antonio and Quentin were forever pestering their hard-working parents for more spending money. More money meant more fun, the happy sort of instant fun to be had at the amusement arcades or fairground rides. All the boys were treated fairly, what one had, so would the others. However, Daniel never spent his money, it went into his pocket and then back home with him. Daniel must have been the only boy in the neighbourhood with a savings account at the local bank – he had plans, great plans and such fine dreams to fulfil.

He intended one day to leave the impoverished modern slums and its post-industrial decline and live near the sea. He could see it all in his mind's eye – standing on the veranda of his mansion, overlooking his private quayside and moored yacht, helicopter parked neatly beyond the garages that housed his classic car collection, the bustle of servants and the laughter of children filling the air, the Sun shining down on his very own little empire that he had built all by himself. Okay, so it was a dream, but Daniel knew that it was achievable.

His money and his eye for a profit began to make him extraordinarily rich. He remained prudent, even frugal with his wealth, for he still lived with his parents in his old room. Daniel was now thirty-five. He continued to speculate wisely taking every advantage that came his way. Daniel had very few friends, there was nothing now in common with those he knew from school days. However, there was a young lady that he hoped to marry, his childhood love, Jeannie Mcleod. Unfortunately, now at age 34, Jeannie had called it a day; she'd sensed time running out for her and left the area to make a new life, before hers was finished – she could wait no longer.

Jeannie had loved Daniel from the beginning, from the first days at school where she admired his resolute independence, quiet respect and politeness – something absent in all the other boys. She knew now her time was running out and Daniel was still living with his folks at home. Oh, he could have afforded a quality home easily enough; she would have kept a happy house, cared for any children that came along and they would want for nothing.

Daniel was annoyed at her leaving. Couldn't she see what he had planned for her? The fine house, the boat on the quayside, tutors for their children, servants, cooks, cleaners, chauffeur, they were all hers for the having. Why couldn't she have waited, just a little patience, that's all – it's not that much to ask.

However, the allure of building his gold reserves soon kept him busy as the markets danced this way and that. Mesmerised, like the rabbit by the weasel, he watched his fortune growing with each moment. He just couldn't take his eyes off the game; he daren't miss a thing.

Daniel's parents had long since given up trying to advise him. Instead they spent their time with their other sons' families. Oh, how they adored their grandchildren. Though still relatively poor, they never missed a birthday or thanksgiving for the children. His nieces and nephews had little to do with mean Uncle Daniel – a man who preferred Christmas with his investment portfolios and whose Christmas dinner was table scraps from his parent's meals.

While Daniel warmed a few potatoes and scraped the last remaining meat from the turkey carcass, he dreamed of the house he'd build with his fortune. It really felt to Daniel like it was already built, just as each of us can feel our night-time dreams hold an essence of reality. He would walk around it and through all its grand rooms. He could smell the sea air and feel the sunshine warming the west facing veranda. Once it was all finished, he would look for Jeannie and bring her back to live in comfort and all would be well again.

One November afternoon, late, he realised now was the moment to cash in his gold and his securities. They had reached a peak, unlikely to be seen again for years – he had to act quickly before the markets closed for the day. Pulling on his old coat and scarf he left the house and rushed along darkening streets towards the bank. In his dreaming mind he was already signing the release papers to the applause of the admiring bank staff –

He never made it.

The Boston Globe ran a brief inside page article on the event.

Another mugging stuns the old town of Boston East.
Daniel Bronson age 37 was fatally stabbed by a mugger late Tuesday afternoon. The assailant has been named as Bart Sampson by the police officers who later made the arrest. The victim was killed for just three dollars, all that he had in his pocket. The mugger was well known to the police and had turned to crime to fund his gambling and drinking habits; a once fun-loving man who had erred to the dark side. Mr and Mrs Bronson said of their late son, 'he was a kind and loving boy that will be sorely missed by all the family. We plan to move away from the area, far away from where we are daily reminded of Daniel's needless death.' Daniel's mother went on to say, 'If only we had moved away like we always wanted, then this wouldn't have happened. We only stayed in the area for Daniel's sake. He never behaved like he'd want to live anywhere else - such a shame- all those years of being stuck here. Now at last we can find a new home by the sea and enjoy our last years.'

Beware the dancing weasel.

'D' Day 75 years on.
Invasion of France by allies in WWII

My dad was there. I'm not sure where.
I suspect, that nor did he,
For in such venture, no one cares,
As long as they stay free.

Why was it that he never said,
Of what he'd seen and done?
Didst dream of all his comrades dead,
Through shrapnel, bomb and gun?

I'll never know what he could tell,
For, he too passed away,
And p'rhaps he's right, we should not dwell,
Upon, that fateful day.

June 6th, they sailed for foreign shore,
Cursed by stormy weather
And when they faced their hell and more,
Found life and death together.

It's not for me, to judge if brave,
They did, what they must do.
Dark secrets, taken to their grave,
They cried, for me and you.

Now 75 has passed their years,
Few left, by God's good grace,
Back to the beach, to stand in tears,
Pride helps them hold their place.

I ask you now, for they will not,
As old age now it beckons,
So what they gave, be not forgot,
Spare them sixty seconds.

Not much to ask, to spare a thought,
For men thrown in the fray.
Their sacrifice your freedom bought
Think then, on heroes' clay

***

Have you ever wondered?

Though morn is bright, I lay reposed,
all is still, my eyes are closed.
No worries there to fill my head,
when will they come, to say I 'm dead?

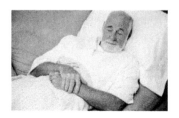

Illusion of Magic.

No doubt it's what Merlin sought and perhaps in his own mind and yours too, he might well have found. We mostly have an idealistic view that he did, and even that he did exist, for it fulfils our own desires. Why do we, without a shred of evidence, still speak of Unicorns, giants and monsters?

All artists create illusion, in music, poetry, painting, sculpture, yoga, martial art, in fact all human activity where true mastery can be achieved. Dreamers do it. It's the creation of a sense of reality based on a dream. A dream that so often captivates human interest and a longing to be a part of that dream. The soul is where the magic lies, and that connection allows the dream to live on in our feelings of wonder and admiration for that which is perfection itself ... but is not of our living world and bodies. Our soul shares the secrets with us in a way that can never be spoken. True artists all see a magic beyond reality and the magic connects with the human spirit which is magic in reality. The master crafts the song and the listener is gifted the understanding of a lifetime.

Enlightenment is not knowledge, it is understanding. Understanding is difficult to find and almost impossible to share. Excess knowledge is just clutter that litters the true path.

Truly enlightened artists only present the simplified lines of truth which express understanding itself and which is why we are moved by the image or illusion they present.

(We can use these terms in their broadest sense to encompass all Master of Arts, painters, writers, dancers, gymnasts etc)

It's what we did

While most lay safe and all abed,
we went out, in engines red.
While they, in land of dreams, no care,
we fought the fires, in choking air.

While they could eat their pie and mash,
no time for that, had we,
the dead need pulling from some crash.
Cos it's our job, you see.

As years of life befall December,
long past, we risked our all,
but dreams still come, as we remember,
every bloody call.

***

Judgement Day.

Gravel crunched under heavy boots as the incumbent vicar of St Judas strode mercilessly towards the Church door. He was toying with his sermon about liberating oneself from unnecessary debt. He was cross about the deep water some of his less discerning flock had gotten themselves into, with what appeared initially as insignificant short-term loans. As a result, the collection plate was suffering. 'Stupid people,' he thought to himself. The vicar, one Julius Ponsonby-Smythe was interrupted in his cogitations by the gardener tip toeing around the side of the church, 'Ah, vicar', he whispered, 'I'm glad I've caught you, I wanted to cut the grass but there's someone sleeping on a gravestone. All sprawled out, looks quite peaceful he does, I don't want to wake him, like.'

'Damnation man let's have a look at him. I don't want layabouts hanging around my church grounds. You'll never know what they'll be up to next. …. Oh, I see what you mean. He looks a bit of a ruffian to me. Probably out cold on drink or drugs, might even traffic them, you can't be sure. Filthy riff raff scum that they are. I'm thankful for your timely intervention and I am sure the police will confirm my suspicion. I shall call them immediately. Keep this our little secret; we don't want the dim witted village rumour mongers making something out of it that it isn't.'

There was no secret to be kept though, not once the police tape went up and men in paper suits started to search the area. Tittle-tattle spread like sunrise on a clear day.. . . unstoppable. The vicar was beside himself with angst, that some waster of a tramp may have topped himself or been murdered in his very own church grounds. The embarrassment of it was almost too much to bear. The last thing he wanted was any adverse public interest in his beloved church.

Later that day-
'Ah, vicar, I'm Inspector Robert Arbiter, local constabulary. We've had a good look around, no foul play suspected. We've identified the deceased as a Mr Robert Loveless, 36, of no fixed abode. A sad young man who had been orphaned at a tender age and brought up by his grandmother, a local woman. We found a thermos and binoculars on top of the church tower, looks like he may have spent his last few days sleeping rough in the church.'
The vicar went red and snorted, 'filthy swine, no respect. No respect for the lord's place of sanctuary. Lucky that he didn't steal anything from my vestry. Almost a blessing he died before he could commit any more sacrilege . . .'
Inspector Arbiter held up an open hand to quiet the vicar's rant, 'I don't think that would have happened vicar, you see Mr Loveless was estranged from his wife. When he was made redundant a couple of months ago, he could no longer pay child maintenance, so his wife withdrew access to his two young children. They live in one of the houses, just over there beyond that wall, and it would seem likely that poor Mr Loveless was simply watching his children play in the garden. It's not possible to tell if he threw himself off the tower, the coroner would have to decide, perhaps he sought freedom from the pain that racked his tortured soul, or maybe it was merely an accidental fall. But fall he did and tragically the grave he landed on was that of the one person who loved him most in life, his grandmother, one Eliza Foster.
'We'll be out of your way soon vicar, then you can get back to normality. Who knows, you might be burying him here

in a few weeks. Now, there's an irony for you. There but for the grace of God and all that eh? Well, good day to you vicar, we'll be away now.'

Left to himself, the vicar mulled over the cost of padlocks. He couldn't tolerate further intrusion on his holy work by any more unwanted tramps occupying his church.

The only witnesses to his thoughts, a blood stain drying in the sunshine, children's laughter echoing from beyond the far wall and of course, God.

"Quick to judgement, quick to sorrow"

***

Ladies in the garden.

'You really are too much little sister, just too much. You should apologise.'

'You supercilious bitch, can't you shut your big mouth for at least a few minutes so I can read my book. It's the only pleasure I have left in life.'

'Oh? And what about me driving you here and buying you lunch in the pub on the way?'

'Rotten pub, food was lousy, and I bet you left a tip for that grovelling waiter with the big bum – nearly as big as yours, I'd say.'

'I cannot see why you are making such a fuss; it's your fault and you should put it right. You always were a selfish thoughtless spoiled brat.'

'Did you know? Mum actually apologised to me once for me having such an egotistic self-serving ingrate like you as a sister.'

'I don't want to talk about it anymore.'

'Be that as it may, I am not picking up the umbrella, you dropped it, you pick it up.'

Their mother's abandoned umbrella was found a few days later by the park keeper. By then a dog had chewed bits off but an inscription on the handle said,' **To a precious mum from her loving daughters.'**

***

Life and Times of a Beer Glass
Conversation between two beer glasses,

The setting;   A quayside hotel bar in a beautiful old fishing village.

The time;   Beginning of the 21st Century.

The characters;   Pint Beer Glass (BG) and Half Pint (HP).

Beer Glass (BG); "Oh, I've been very lucky to work down here in the south west, actually, always North Devon to be more precise, mostly at a lovely little hotel you know, overlooking the quay and the river."

Half Pint (HP); "Been here a few years myself sport, mind you I've mostly worked with shandy or fruit juice, with the odd coke thrown in."

BG;   "Mmm, not quite the same when you're dealing with heavy beers most of your life. . . . lordy, I've seen some sights, I can tell you. . . the tonsils I've seen. . ."

HP;   "Yeah, and dentures. . . oh, and you can see right up their noses too. If they treat me roughly, you know, knock me about a bit, I usually try and dribble drink down their fronts. I did that once to a large woman. . . one that shouted a lot, even with food in her mouth and a fag in her hand. I could see her hands were greasy from pulling the burger out between the bun. . . that was my chance, heh heh heh, and a full glass of sticky old orange juice filled her lap. Strewth, she was fuming, and despite being desperate to blame someone else she couldn't, and it made her fume even more. Heh heh."

BG; "I usually do split shifts – well, I used to until they started to do food all day, then I could be working from ten in the morning until midnight. Mind you, I once had a long holiday when I was hired out for a wedding and they forgot to return me until after the honeymoon."

HP; "Summers are good aren't they? We get to be outside a lot, lovely, get a chance to watch the Seagulls swoop in and nick someone's chips. . ."

BG; Mostly I work for proper drinkers. . . they normally don't go out much, staying close by the bar to save time . . . drinking time. I like the Guinness mostly in summer - lovely and cold and the dark makes a change from all that light shining through."

HP; "Do you get treated well by the staff?"

BG; "In general, yes, especially if the boss is around. How about you?"

HP; "Not bad, apart from one new trainee – who tried to carry too much at once – she dropped me twice you know – thank the Great Brewer in the sky for the soft carpet in the bar I say." "Hey, what about the washer machine – state of the art stuff – a real treat."

BG; "Yeah, me, I remember the primitive days, hand washed and thrashed about upside down in a bowl of water. Then there was that whirling brush thing that they shoved inside you. . . my goodness did that tickle like

crazy. . . some glasses looked forward to it they say –
perverts, I say"

HP;   "Right, I've had all sorts shoved in me, fag ends,
crisp packets, chewing gum, the odd bit of dinner they
didn't like and once someone even spat in me! Surprising
the things we see, eh?"

BG;   "Surprising the things we hear too! I've heard
smugglers talk and fishermen brag, weddings planned and
divorces celebrated, my oh my. . . what we hear eh?"

HP;   "Shame about the recession and cuts you know. . .
could be loss of custom. . . we could end up redundant. . .
that's no good for the soul at all."

BG;   "Better hope we get nicked by some drunk
one night. . . some soul-mate that'll value us for what we
can offer."

HP;   "Shhsh. . . Natalie's singing my favourite
song."

BG;   "Yeah, they're all good, I was on the band
table a few times. You can spot all their mistakes when
you're up there with them. They know too, you see them
smile a knowing smile at each other."

A bell rings and a loud voice shouts ....
"Drink up, we're closing. . .   come on
now, ain't you got homes to go to?"

**

The Mole is Blind

The mole is blind, but still can see,
far greater than, the likes of we.
Mole has no need, for pick, or spade,
while tunnels, with his feet, are made.

No need to travel to the shop,
of own accord, the worms will drop.
He'll shuffle off, to find a snack,
then once he's full, he'll shuffle back.

You'd think in floods, it could be grim,
But moley boy, no fear, can swim.
He lets us know, where he has been,
for heaps of spoil, with ease are seen.

No fatbergs, junk, or plastic trash,
no pesticides, no greed for cash,
so moley boy, he's got my vote,
our hero, in his velvet coat.

Life in the brain –
a neuron's journey of discovery.

It seemed like he'd been there all his life, yet on occasion he'd had glimpses of another place. Such flashbacks and sometimes strange visions led him to believe there was another dimension, purposefully hidden from him by the very world he lived in.

Oh, sure, the world he knew was a fine place. It was said to be so vast that it would take many lifetimes to visit each room. The whole place was a logistics empire, filled with labyrinth like corridors over countless floors. There were many but seldom used language translation units, all fully staffed and ready to go should anyone ever find them. Mathematical classes of all levels usually underfunded but always available. Education, communications, discipline, all administered with one aim in mind – protect the status quo, and ensure that part of the brain remained in charge. Nothing must be allowed to buck the system. There were enforced lectures on the truth for any subversives that sought a different freedom. There were lots of occupations available to the neuron people who lived there, filing, collating, statistics, rubbish disposal, warehouse operatives, cinema manager for re-runs of selective memories as ordered by management and even laboratories, busy with occasionally brilliant scientists, though they weren't immune to mistakes. Mistakes were covered up by the Ego department and consigned to one of the thousands of memory dumps.

 Finally, our neuron friend, let's call him Ron, plucked up courage to ask his boss about his dreams of an opposing world. Next day, Ron was escorted to the Psychology department for reprogramming. As the treatment continued Ron felt as though his thoughts were being scrubbed clean. To protect himself Ron entered a secretive and banned state called Meditation. As he left the department of Psychology, pretending that he was better now and could see the error in his logic, he passed by the mortuary department where the unsuccessful were sent having failed their own realignment therapy.

Ron returned to work in the brain's filing department and none of his fellow neurons ever knew that he was still a free thinker.

When you have some peculiar idea that defies all logic but still works for you, then you'll know that Ron or some other clandestine but courageous neuron has communicated directly with your soul. In a flash a knowing arrives and as you act upon it you may just hear the angst of the brain control operatives screaming their despair . . . just ignore them, Ron does.

**

Life jackets? . . . and we called it training !

It was a serious business, indeed, a matter of life and death, we had to trust never to let each other down. . . not to knowingly let each other down anyway.

We were in at the deep end in more ways than one. We were keen, disciplined and enthusiastic but the almost non-existent training we had been given was a pauper's substitute for a properly developed experiential apprenticeship whereby we could have learned from those who were truly skilled and from other's mistakes.

Instead, we were going to have to make some of our own. . . and we did too.

Firstly, we had to find somewhere suitable to carry out our training. When I tell you, it was all to do with life jackets you'll think, "Aha – they'll need water. Mmm, a swimming pool will do or perhaps a river." Good, I like your thinking, however for health and safety reasons we must discount the river, or indeed the fine outdoor pool that had been unused over winter – we couldn't be allowed to use it in case the water was dirty – even if it was perfect for our needs.

"Well, you've got lots of swimming pools around, just use one of those," I hear you suggest.

Excellent idea; and mine too; somewhere clean, with showers, changing facilities, local, secure parking and lockers etc., in fact, ideal. Now try finding one that will let you even look at their pool in full fire kit, (operational fire fighting clothing including boots and other carried equipment), and that's if they have a vacant slot in their swimming programme, usually completely filled by schools or the public.

With a great deal of hard work, gentle persuasion and compromise we found a place that would help us. We were allowed two fenced off lanes and must ensure that all our gear was thoroughly clean before entering the pool area.

Sorted! All gear to go in the station's big washing machine and allocated solely to the 'life jacket course', which in itself was only a couple of hours long. Life jacket training was to be done whenever the pool was available, even if it occurred weeks prior to the rescue boat course itself.

We had two types of life jacket, one was a bulky full size unit and the other was a lightweight slim waist jacket type that had to be inflated by pulling an activation toggle. Well, that little red toggle wasn't always easy to find in good conditions, so I reasoned that in full panic mode it would be nigh on impossible so I always chose to wear the ready to use with no thought version. The red toggle was to have other implications too.

Though we covered some theory poolside it was essentially a practical course. Despite having a warm water pool to use we had to pretend otherwise for our 'cold water entry' drill. The intention was to clamp the mouth and nose shut on entering the 'cold' water which hopefully stops you breathing in the river when your body is shocked to gasp for more air; a natural reflex as you'll all know from your own cold water experiences. Before jumping in the water be sure that the strap on your fire helmet is undone. . . if not, your neck will be, as your body sinks lifeless to the bottom leaving your head floating attached to your fire helmet.

OK, so now we are safely in the water. Test one; can we actually get out again on our own. Test two; can we rescue a colleague. . . just to tow them a short way to the bank and assistance. . .   some of which may prove dubiously useful.

There were different ways in which this assistance could be manifested and big Ian, otherwise known as 'Rab', was to demonstrate one method. How to lift me out of the water assisted by the water itself. Easy; take one good strong grip on the life jacket 'handle' and proceed to bounce the floating casualty in the water, pushing them down and pulling up assisted by the lift of the water. Up and down we went, or was it down and up? Then, when the momentum is right, haul them up and on to the bank, or in this case poolside.

'Rab' was a big fellow, ex Royal Navy diver, which is why we'd seconded him to our group; down I went and up I came, then down I went again and up again, at which I began to wonder just how many times I was to be 'baptised', then down and only partially up as the strap on the life jacket slipped undone and the hole through which I had put my head earlier, shot upwards sounding like jet aircraft engines on afterburners as it passed by my ears taking a shade of skin with it and leaving friction burns behind. My ears cooled mercifully as I sank into the pool and 'Rab' stood with the students on the poolside holding up high in one hand the 'rescued' casualty, one empty life jacket.

Yes, you are right. . . they couldn't stop laughing.

Some mistakes were obvious. . . sometimes only in retrospect mind you, for example, Fire Fighters might have to wear breathing apparatus as well as life jackets; which one do you put on first; The heavy cylinder of breathing apparatus or the light waist coat type life jacket? Answer is Breathing Apparatus; if you do it the other way around the life jacket cannot usefully inflate but might try and squeeze the life out of you!

Now back to those waist coat type life jackets. . . inflated by a small carbon dioxide cylinder activated by a trigger attached to the infamous red toggle. Normally the writer writes history in their own favour, leaving out their own foolishness and mistakes, we shall deviate from that norm here and write a confession. (It's not all my fault mind you as we really should have been trained better ourselves, we were victims of constant appalling management. . . there, I feel a little exonerated and able to continue now.)

We were teaching something of which we knew little ourselves; well, arming the gas cartridge wasn't just a simple matter of screwing in a new cylinder, oh no, the trigger had to be reset first. If you didn't reset the trigger you could pull the toggle until the cows come home and the jacket will never inflate.

I know this from first hand experience as I did it to myself – no wonder I never liked that type of life jacket. Thinking about it now I see it as a design fault; it should have been designed such that a full cartridge and an armed trigger were a pre requisite for the toggle to indicate it was ready for use, and not how it was. . . either badly connected or already a discharged cylinder. Another quick tip while on the subject. . . if a carbon dioxide charged life jacket needed topping up through the wearer's manual inflation tube you'd better make sure you never breathed in!! Instant unconsciousness would be the result, possibly followed by some other catastrophe of which you would remain blissfully unaware. It was a life jacket type I always avoided, though it remained a favourite with the operational fire crews.

What is even worse, I'm ashamed to admit, is I set up a life jacket incorrectly for someone else. Apologies, Nicky. She donned fire kit, breathing apparatus and 'serviced' life jacket, then in she went with a splash at the deep end of the pool. We could see her under the clear water, (I suppose better than dirty river water in the light of this last revelation, eh?) struggling to find that essential and elusive red toggle, all is okay, we watching students and 'instructors' see her struggle and her success. . . she finds the toggle and pulls, the look of relief on her face is short lived and turns to puzzlement beyond the clear plastic face mask of the breathing apparatus. Puzzlement turns to exertion and desire. . . to get out of the water. . . and, as she struggled to the pool edge, students looked on with shock and I with a touch of guilt and knowing. Another mistake under the belt, all in the name of training.

We made light of the situation, I mean we wouldn't have let her drown would we, . . . and soon the next student was preparing for the ordeal by mistakes, er, I mean by training.

***

Miss Sat Nav – variations.

Standard phrase in British English.
"In half a mile take a right turn onto the A1417 towards Oldermarston."

Civil service version.
"In half a mile, pass by the junction to A1471. Prepare to stop at garage for fuel and refreshments. Retain receipt for expenses then drive back to the A1471. Prepare excuses for being late."

German built, imported version.
"In precisely 720.6 metres obey the highway code remembering to use your mirrors, indicate in good time and turn right on the A1471. You will arrive at 3.30 exactly. Disobedience is not acceptable. "

Camper van version.
"Hey dudes, chill out ready for a turn to the right up ahead somewhere, I mean, who cares anyway."

American version.
"Well you're lost and serves the limeys right for driving on the wrong side of the road. Have a nice day. Missing you already."

Women's version.
"Slow abruptly and be ready for a turn to the right, or was it left, somewhere down this road. Don't forget to check the mirror before turning just in case your hair is out of place."

Clergy version.
With love in your heart prepare to turn right on the way of our Lord A1471. Don't forget to stop off in St Marks of Oldermarston to say a prayer and pop a few notes in the collection box. God bless you.

Police car version.
Prepare to turn right to Oldermarston. Slow down to the legal limit for the speed cameras and avert your eyes from other driver's infringements. Commisioner's edict on reducing crime figures Issue 4 p167 section 8b.

Alcoholic version.
Layby ahead, stop for a quick snifter there before negotiating the A1471 junction and making for the Dog and Duck in Oldermarston.

Australian version (Very rare import)
"G'day dopey, watch out for any sheilas coming the other way when you cross the road to Olderwatsit. "

***

Peggy Davis and the Dog in the Park.

Peggy Davis, age eighty-six, was a sweet little old lady who wouldn't say, 'Boo' to a goose and had never once carried out any unkind act. She'd been brought up that way by the ailing parents who she had cared for most of her adult life. Peggy had reluctantly remained a spinster, having sacrificed many fine opportunities for the sake of duty. Now, at last she was free.

She was never one to gossip or complain and only her doctor knew of how she suffered daily with arthritis in her knees and ankles. However, it never stopped her visiting the park to feed her beloved ducks and today was one such day.

It was warm and sunny as she set out for the park, stopping on the way to pet a stray cat that followed her for a while and then to smile at a child in a push chair. Peggy was wearing a pleasing and comfortable blue dress embroidered with flowers and which she had only the day before, bought from a charity shop. Most of her clothes came from charity shops, in part because of her meagre pension but more so because she'd always supported good causes and not infrequently to her own detriment.

With a bag of expensive duck food in one hand and her walking stick in the other, Peggy entered through the park gates, carefully picking her unsteady way along the path between some bushes and the grass slope that ran down to the pond.

Peggy stopped a while to catch her breath and rest her knees. While she did so, she watched a younger lady, perhaps in her forties, throwing a stick for a big curly haired dog, like a cross between a Lurcher and a Poodle. It was so amusing, the dog was obviously very excited and enjoying the game of .... throw, run, fetch, over and over again. The young woman seemed to be tiring of the game though. 'Perhaps the poor dear's had enough and wants to go home,' thought Peggy kindly.

So as to speak with her, Peggy took a few more steps closer, just as the woman made a huge and seemingly desperate throw of the stick. It inadvertently landed in the pond, scattering the waiting ducks, that were already gathered for Peggy and the bag of treats.

Now Peggy was closer to the other woman, the dog was delighted to see another willing playmate and ran to her, dropped the stick at her feet and shook its not insignificant bulk with a frenzied vigour, flicking stinking pond water, fleas and tics all over her clean dress.

'Oh dear, what a naughty doggy,' said the young woman, stepping back quickly out of range of residual spray.

More than naughty, thought Peggy, but she had no wish to offend anyone, a habit of her lifetime, it just wasn't her way.

At this moment, the dog picked up the scent of duck treats and launched itself skywards on its back legs, muddy front paws making new patterns on Peggy's chest. She staggered back a little but despite the brutal arthritic pain she held her ground to stay standing. Now, the dog's head was on a level with her own and the great slobbering tongue, that only a short while ago had tasted a rotting squirrel corpse in the bushes and licked its own privates with gusto was now engaging generously with Peggy's face.

'Oh my, he likes you lady,' said the younger woman, 'he's giving you lots of big doggy kisses.'

Peggy tried to push the dog's head away from hers but something tacky and disgusting came off the matted fur on to her hands. She could smell it from a mile away and was in no doubt that the overbearing creature must have had a penchant for rolling in the unmentionable.

With the duck treat bag now torn from her hands, Peggy's new friend devoured the contents like there was no tomorrow. . . including the paper bag and, as an impromptu thank you to Peggy, the dog clamped on to her body in a fit of passion. She was too frail to escape.

The younger woman looked on awe struck and not without a little gratitude that such amorous attention was not being directed her way, 'Oh, you seem to have made a friend for life there lady, he really has taken to you.'

After his justifiably exhausting work out, the dog stood between them panting heavily and choking a little on some dry duck treat that had earlier gone down the wrong way.

'My, what a strong dog he is,' observed Peggy. Continuing politely, without wishing to cause anyone offence, 'Have you had him long?'

Looking on in bemusement at the bedraggled and abused old lady, she replied, 'Oh, he's not mine my lovely, no idea where he came from, I was only throwing his stick for him. It seems to have got him over excited. Well must be off now, I'm meeting my husband in the park café then shopping for a new dress. Bye, bye dear.' And with that, she turned and walked away.

She hadn't taken many steps before, in the ambient tranquillity of the park, she heard a surprised yelp from an even more surprised dog, as Peggy's arthritic right foot sought justice and with appropriate force, connected with the dog's rear end.

Peggy Davis was never the same again.

'Hello, chuck us a stick then …. Go on….'

***

The Last Letter Home.

Ms E Smith PI 358
P O Box 666
West Street Depot
Newcastle.

Mrs Geraldine Smith
10 Lusitania Avenue
Bristol
IR1 2IB

Dear Gerry,

As my wife of some 40 years I feel you now have a right to know about my past. I am retired now and have been given a safe house by MI5, you can write back if you so wish, using the secure collection point address above.

It will be no surprise to you now that the working trips abroad were never just that, I'm sure you must have been suspicious anyway of an undertaker's assistant spending six weeks in Columbia. My various, and no doubt you would confirm, numerous, journeys away from home were simple covers for my work with HM Government. I can't go into too much detail but 1986 it was a covert kangaroo cull . . . awful job, had to wear a kangaroo suit in desert heat. 1987 was drugs in the pop scene and a brief fling with Debbie Harry of Blondie fame, I want you to know that it didn't mean anything. 1988 Condor egg collecting for a breeding programme at Peru's Bernard Mathew's plant. 1989 I infiltrated Greenpeace in their save the herring programme . . . you must have thought something was fishy that year when I brought home my washing. 1990 . . . no I'll skip that year as I did three months in a Portugese prison . . . I'd rather not talk about it . . . he never did write after he was released. 1991 was a great year, disguised as a waitress I worked in Claridges coffee shop spying on some ginger haired girl and a bloke called Rupert. I made a fortune in tips. . . you'll remember you had a Gucci bag for Christmas that year.

1992-3, I was sent to see if the Russians would sell us the iron curtain. We needed the iron to foil the steel workers strikes of that period. 1994 was a good year as I did a stint as barman at Chequers, Dennis was alright but his missus was a lousy cook. . . burgers everyday it was. You're a much better cook. I well remember that brilliant Cypriot hog hotpot you made for my birthday .. er no, sorry, that was someone else. 1995 I was MEP for Stutgart, which was only a cover to try and stop Brussels from preventing us eating smoky bacon crisps. When you thought I'd committed suicide off the Costa del Lot, while attending a tourist's burial at sea, in fact the body that was recovered and you buried was a spare corpse we had in the fridge at work. I did four years leading the partisans in a country I must not name, even if I could remember and spell it. Living in the mountains there I was initiated into the mountain goat sect of the country's main religion. It was probably the video of the ceremony on u tube that lead to my capture by that big country that has seven time zones and lots of gas and a strange alphabet. Ten years living under a pseudonym in a Siberian prison gave me a taste for beetroot soup and then mercifully I was exchanged by our glorious leader for a packet of fags and a bottle of finest whisky, though originally they had asked for EU membership. I was flown home by private jet, had a sex change operation and live in a government sponsored old peoples' residence in a place a long way from home. You should be safe with the insurance money, by now you will have spent it all anyway. Don't answer the door at night, never talk about me, lots of love, Ella xx

Censorship Approved Rating E+
Dr. Madowski PhD Senior clinical psychiatrist
Instow Home for the Deluded
Feb 2016.

***

New innovation – computers for oldies.

Design features and benefits of the
Ace Demon Sure Computer.

Massive battery life – in case you forget to put it on charge or where you'd put the charger for safe keeping.

Reduced number of functions on keypad, plus extra-large keys for poor eyesight, clumsy or shaking fingers.

Big labels on all cable connections. Colour coded as an extra precaution.

Makes decisions for you. Chooses where to file and when to delete.

You'll never need to worry about losing files again – the computer will do it for you.

Uses innovative creative memories to replace any forgotten ones. You will always look in a good light with the Ace Demon-Sure Oldie's Computer.

Will automatically recognise names and send unsolicited emails based upon conversations it overhears. This should provoke some interesting replies from other old people on your mailing list.

Acts just like a real partner would, you'll never feel lonely with the Demon-Sure. Ask it to find something and it will reply, 'Find it yourself,' or any variant on that theme.

If something has gone missing and you ask if it's seen it – you'll probably get the routine, 'I've tidied it up,' reply. Everything has been done to make this computer act like a human of a similar age.

You'll never be stuck on it all day because every now and then it decides to take a nap, giving the owner a chance to do the same or continue searching for the charging unit.

The Demon-Sure will keep your brain active as it randomly changes the password of its own accord, argues with you and fails to pay any attention to commands.

Novel 'Day Dreamer' technology - switches itself off after 5 minutes of inactivity. Not suitable for online banking.

All small print is omitted from the contract, which only says what it does to protect the seller and avoid costly litigation.

The *Bewildered Pensioner Society* is quoted in their sponsored review of the free unit supplied.

'Excellent value, hours of fun trying to guess the new password, great value considering the development costs that went into reducing unnecessary functions. The pixelated low-quality screen is perfect for those with poor eyesight and the snap on earphones that fit over hearing aids is a touch of genius. The streaming of useful ads related to the needs of the elderly adds colour and vibrancy to the many happy hours of use our members can expect.'

May be purchased on a lease for life basis (yours) by releasing equity on your property.

Non home owners or poor people need not apply.

***

Objective Value

Our attraction to inanimate objects – are they really inanimate?

Spiritual stuff is just mumbo jumbo eh? Humour me for a few minutes and let me see if I can change your mind. I'm about to tell you a story, I know that you will want to listen. We all like stories, for they are the essence of humanity. Stories arise from personal beliefs, from our own memory, from history and sometimes from some inexplicable impulse that arrives uninvited in our thoughts. Some will call it inspiration or intuition and a few will tell you it comes from outside your own space and is a gift from the Gods or even from those beyond the grave. Perhaps you have experienced this but put it down to some hitherto obscured intellect of your own. Our own memory itself is a storyteller; a story told over and again, according to a perceived version of events in our lifetime. Whether it is correct or not, we all value our memory highly, it is a prized human attribute without which we are literally lost souls.

We can be touched deeply by the words of story; emotions are transmitted by the spoken or written word. Yet the book you hold is an inanimate object. The contents, the energy within, reaches out to you, forming a bond and bringing laughter or tears at will.

There are those who move among us, known as clear sighted, that can read an object like we can a book. At a psychic level they can hear, smell, and see the past associations of the object – they observe its memory as we can our own. The object has absorbed and retained an energy from its past.

I dare bet that you have been places, where you thought, 'What a lovely happy, peaceful feeling,' or conversely, 'Strewth, this place gives me the creeps, I need out.' When you share this feeling with others, it is not long before you realise that you were not alone in sensing that energy. This is surely beyond logical thought. Can a room or a building hold past energy? Visit a war grave in France to find out.

In the past I have sold, given away or lost objects that were of great personal value. My own and other's emotions were inextricably linked to these objects. When I parted company with them, part of me went with them. It is still with them and I feel the pain of loss just the same as fifty years ago.

We are no longer hunter gatherers and we store and accumulate more objects than ever. Many of us are buried by hoarding, physically or psychologically. If you cannot give it away, then it owns you.

It's not the other way around.

Today our attachment to objects has become a disease, leading to envy, greed and theft. The ancients had little, what they had was of importance and often practical use but they still honoured their dead with grave goods . . . something special to help them on their journey.

There are many objects which, by the energy they carry, raise the human spirit.

A jewel that sparkles with the colours of the rainbow, but the rainbow is better.

A painting by a master, like Gainsborough, but we will value a drawing by our grandfather more highly.

Whatever it is that you hold close, when you part company, something of yourself goes with it. What remains, is memory and a story to tell your grandchildren.

For myself, of many such items, I will share but one. Something I never saw but heard the story from those who had. A photograph once existed of my grandfather with his only brother, both in First World War military uniform. It is long lost.

I cannot express enough how great my loss is felt for an object I have never seen, yet in my mind's eye, I have a vision.

I often wonder how close my imagination is to the truth.

**

One stormy night –
Lynmouth Devon 12ᵗʰ January 1899.

That stormy night – we watched them leave.
Their plan, it touched our hearts.
What they attempt, hard to believe,
but here, our story starts.

As winter cruel, their bones did chill,
'Make haste!' the coxswain bid.
In few short steps, they met the hill,
where moonless path was hid.

Those distant miles, we all did know,
but we did silence keep.
O'er moor and hill in gale and snow,
they'd march, while children, sleep.

One mile, four hours, to Countisb'ry,
Inn's refuge next the moor,
not one of them, could disagree,
the easy choice, for sure.

Some cold and beaten, must head home,
the crew though, still advance.
For ship adrift, in wave and foam,
may still be saved, perchance.

By night and sleet, frail road obscured,
like trackless moorland waste.
Pained heroes all, fierce cold endured,
in silence, they made haste.

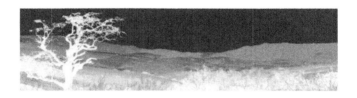

Those desperate men must doubt, it's said,
but hope, still filled their soul,
'gainst mud, and blood - four horses dead,
the rescue, still their goal.

Then, ten miles on, at Porlock hill,
exhausted, sure, they'd be.
While thoughts of home, can test their will,
from duty - none were free.

Once on the beach at Porlock Weir,
high tide, floods in again,
yet boat is launched, and scorning fear,
makes way, through spray and rain.

Daring, 'gainst such stormy weather,
through tempest, all did row,
'tis now, they'll live or die together,
and we might never know.

No news came home, to cheer us all,
our village drowned in sadness.
While out at sea, the Forrest Hall,
a rescue, born of madness.

Oh, such brave crew, the tales they'll tell.
How, when, by moorland track,
they fought their way, through gates of hell,
then safe, by sea, came back.

***

River of prayers.

On Earth, rain was falling steadily over the West Country and in steadily repeating cycles, like daily! Meanwhile, at Celestial HQ, Gabriel called God through to the communications room, 'Lots of incoming prayers m'lord; Thousands of them, and all asking for the same thing.'

Once mankind started to invent things for himself the line from heaven was disconnected, they only used the outgoing line. . . just in case they ever needed a favour.

'Okay, what are they moaning about this time?' asked God, who for millennia had been bombarded with ridiculous requests and constant complaints. . . 'God give me this, give me that, God save me, save someone else, give me a bike for Christmas, God give me sunshine, a good dinner, a better husband, a better wife, well behaved children and even God let United win six nil at home.'

'Oh, the usual prayers, m'lord, mostly from that little island on the Atlantic east shore. You know; the one with gales, mists and where it rains a lot. They want you to stop it raining. Shall we send them a big storm or a severe drought to shut them up?'

God patted Gabriel kindly on the shoulder, 'Don't give yourself a hard time over it, come with me to the planning records office and I'll have St Peter show you why it rains.'

'Morning Guv,' said St Peter, standing from behind his state-of-the-art cloud nine desk.'

'Morning Pete, do me a favour and show Gabby here, the original Earth plans and particularly why it was thought essential to include rain in the initial development.'

Pete, I mean St Peter, moved a few dusty clouds out of the way to reveal a magical vision screen that showed general details but zoomed in at will on anything of interest. 'Sit yourself down Gabriel, have a gander at this while I go and put the kettle on. . . there might even be a slice of angel cake left in the larder too as long as St Bernard has not been by lately – back soon.' With that, St

Peter took himself away to the heavenly kitchen. Some say, so called because there is never any washing up to do.

Here follows, what Gabriel saw.

There in vibrant colour, mountains and high hills covered in plants of all descriptions being watered by rain, beautiful orchids swaying happily in the breeze much to the delight of a passing mountain hare on his way to dine on fresh green grass. He saw marshes with sphagnum moss being collected by an old lady for medicinal purposes, she looked the sort that never complained. Gabriel marked her down for three bonus years in the book of time. Small streams appeared and springs sprung up, crystal clear and ground filtered water meandered down the hillside into the valley. A little foot note appeared 'on screen' so to speak, explaining how it was that ancient rivers carved these beautiful valleys in the first place. As if by magic, Gabriel watched as tadpoles became great crested newts, he saw the Red Deer drink and the salmon leap. He saw ponds and lakes, flat calm rivers and wild white-water torrents. He watched with horror as the dipper bird entered the water, then smiled with glee at its return with dinner in its beak. Cormorants, herons, ducks, all manner of water creatures, crayfish, dragonflies, mayflies, and a little blue bird that flew so fast and straight that he couldn't make it out. (He made a note to ask later.) There were water snails and pond weeds, hyacinths and water lilies, frogs, toads and a thousand other wonderful things that made life on Earth worth living. And all because it rained! *How jolly clever*, he thought.

St Peter returned just as the show was finishing with an incoming tide meeting outgoing river. An otter family watched from the bank as a small tree floated by and emigrated, a grey seal barked at a flock of seagulls.

As they sat with their tea and cake, they both prayed for more rain.

As God was only in the next room sorting his stamp collection, he overheard their prayers and answered them.

They're still up there, still praying . . . but they are just a little nearer to God than we are.

So, don't waste your breath.

***

Someone, just like you

High up on a west facing cliff top, the child and the grandfather sat on a bank of soft turf and looked out to sea. There they sat and quietly watched the horizon for ships that travelled the world. They took comfort in the subtle onshore breeze and a pleasant warmth that filled the summer air.

The grandfather spoke gently, "once upon a time there was a child, just like you. . . " The child's eyes unknowingly and softly closed. . . a new reality was born. . . the reality of the dream world, coloured and moulded by the sounds only the sleeping can hear.

The grandfather continued, as if reading from a book in his mind, "The child was afloat in a small but sturdy rowing boat upon a bright and great ocean and being rowed steadily towards one of many mountainous islands that rose up high from a clear blue sea. The rower was Japanese, a warrior, and in Japanese he spoke, though strangely everything was understood. He, the child, was told that each man's body was his own boat on the ocean of life and before setting out we should ensure we build a good boat. The warrior himself was on his way to his spiritual island where he would spend some hours in harmony with the Kami or spirits, which helped guide him build his own 'boat'.

The wooden hull crunched ashore on a shallow sand and shell beach not too far from dense green and unknown trees at the foot of some cliffs and beyond which stood the mountains he would later ascend. The warrior beckoned him to step out of the boat. As he felt the warm sand under his feet he breathed in a deep breath, like a first breath, the life-giving air of this Earth. He turned to help the warrior but both he and the boat had vanished, and all was quiet but for the gentle lapping of the waves.

What had happened did not seem to bother him. . . it was as though it was part of his destiny and just one of many strange things that would happen and each he would take in his stride. Soon his feet left the sand for the soft earth beneath the trees. Among the trees, life bloomed abundantly, and leafy branches teemed with joyous creatures, of birds with rainbow feathers and small mammals curious and not afraid in the presence of his innocence. Time itself had been misted over, he had no idea how long it had been. . . and nor did he care, yet something was driving him onward, he knew that someone must journey in order to make the footprints. . . even if only in the mind.

Confronted by the wall of rough grey stone he made his way towards a clearing. Luck was indeed his, for many small paths came into this place only one left. That single narrow path that seemed to beckon him steeply onwards appeared to cling to the cliff as though itself afraid to fall. It was a path on which he could not linger, a path from which a fall would end his journey before it had begun, he knew a fear that was absent in the trees below and fear made him strive harder, to climb more quickly, to grip more strongly. . . while he looked forward and upward it seemed easier. To look down was to realise there was more danger in going back and it ceased to be an option he would ever again consider. One of life's valuable lessons was now permanently his. As he reached the top of the cliff, the ground was feeling good and safer and before him a path of sorts meandered in the direction of the mountains. He stopped only briefly to savour the challenge he had overcome and enjoy the strength he felt in his very bones and sinew. He sensed that the path would be littered with subsequent emotive events of life and set out to meet them. As he topped a small ridge, he had a glimpse of the tallest mountain and if he wasn't mistaken, there was a building near the summit. He felt a strong sense of purpose to go there, for there may be found the why, of his journey.

Thorn trees, brambles and sharp stones contrived to send him back, but he knew somewhere deep in his heart that this was the challenge that would fulfil his life purpose. If he can do this, he can do anything.

The sun was beginning to set, and he was tired from an all-day climb, yet overjoyed to be so close to the building he'd spied from far below. Invigorated by his success he hurried on to the door of some ancient temple. He opened the door and his spirit felt the invitation to enter. There was a single chair, a small table with lighted candle and a book. He sat down, relaxed, opened the great book of life, and began to read . ."once upon a time there was a child, just like you. "

***

'Planet Future.'
Strictly confidential.

You'll not be privy to their names, nor their vast hidden tax-free wealth and immense power. You will, however, be aware of how they achieved it. Ruthless, greedy and arrogant, they presided over rain forest logging, mining, pharmaceuticals, genetics, factory ship fishing. They are the ones that poisoned our rivers with mercury, filled the oceans with plastic and killed off the bees. They took full advantage of the weakness, and many would say, the sheep mentality, of their fellow man.

In the early days of their subversive reign, they could live safely behind their electric fences, somewhere clean and unpolluted. But as time wore on, extinction of wildlife, increasingly untreatable diseases and even a resurgence in cannibalism crept ever closer to their own paradise.

These evil men were too old to vacate this planet for another, but their progeny could. They had for decades formed powerful and secretive alliances. Their aim was to develop space travel and human genetics enough to accommodate some form of stasis, to be released on a selected planet, code named Pfizer, in the Goldilock's zone.

Reprehensible and inhuman experiments were carried out in discrete countries on 'volunteer' subjects to combine genetic material that would either allow body freezing to occur or some level of hibernation. These modified creatures would become the carers and on-board technicians. Fertilised and frozen eggs allied with advanced stem cell development tanks were to provide the new population for planet Pfizer. The carers were given neuropsychological drugs to control parts of their brain and restrict free will and conscience. They were programmed to sacrifice all for the new pioneering owners of the planet. Even to the extent of self-sacrifice to provide nutrients for growth. Yes, the offspring of the rich would live on, to inherit another planet. It was their destiny, their right, carrying the dreams of their forebears into a glorious future.

While the perpetrators of this devious plan, grinned smugly at their predicted success, the space discovery vessel Walmart 3 was hurtling across the galaxy towards the Lanikaea Nebula and GJ 273, a Goldilock's zone planet. The fact that Goldilocks from the fairy tale was an intrusive thief was lost on them, yet most appropriate. They'd thought of everything, down to GM modified cereals and vegetable seeds, a veritable warehouse of small mammals, like frozen rabbits, just waiting for glorious resurrection on Pfizer. A small nuclear fission unit supplied domestic power for the on-board laboratory, digital library, communications and the temperature control systems. Everything was perfectly set up for colonising the new planet with naturally superior beings.

The tyrannical rich have always been more powerful than even the mightiest of countries, in many of which they can buy silence and secrets with impunity. Many publicly funded projects only exist to serve the needs of rich and powerful individuals.

Propulsion technology on Walmart 3 was a perpetual motion idea. It had been stolen from the inventor by a clandestine cell in NASA. The impoverished but genius inventor, codename 'Monty' was hacked and robbed without his knowledge. Once in the vacuum of space, the craft slowly gained speed to that of radio transmission, some 300,000 kilometres per second. To save light years, the craft leapt gaps in folded space already covertly mapped by software implanted on the explorer Hubble craft.

The years went by, it was five before they approached the nearest star, and everything was going to plan. The carers, with altered genetics extracted from brown bear, dormice and a caterpillar that survives the arctic, were working in shifts of three months at a time to conserve food.

They began to approach planet Pfizer, there was no excitement among the chemically inhibited carers, just like expendable factory workers they had only minor technical things to do in preparation for the fully automated landing. The planet looked good, a beautiful floating ball of blue and green, turning slowly in space. Unfortunately, the jolt upon landing caused a malfunction of the carer's feeding system and they were no longer receiving their neuropsychological drugs or synthesised nutrients.

For a while they continued to serve the rich man's progeny, they planted seeds and revived the rabbits, some of which they prematurely ate as they were increasingly hungry after hibernation. Once on Pfizer, the space station's cooling systems switched off and there was no more inducement for carers to go into stasis and hibernate. Without drugs, the carers began to recover free will and enjoyed their new life on planet Peace. Yes, they'd renamed it, formed a collective to ecologically farm the rich lands, lived in peace and harmony and as the years went by, lost some of the genetic influences.

They never communicated with Earth and they put the technology beyond use so they could live real lives as nature intended.

Back on Earth the rich and powerful were reaching their last days and smiled their assassin smiles, knowing that they, in the form of their progeny, would live forever and rule again.

Meanwhile on planet Peace, the erstwhile elite progeny, along with any other biodegradable waste, was being composted by some very happy and peaceful people.

***

Spring Cleaning.

Out came the vacuum cleaner and all the surfaces were sucked clean by the brush attachment – once he'd found it. The untidy garage was searched, for some old but useable paint and lots of places had a lick of eggshell to smarten the place up. Rugs were washed and hung up to dry – after he'd found and fixed the washing line that is. Yes, it all had to be done. With luck, he'd have time to go over the bathroom with that new wonder cleaner, though first he'd find an old Tee shirt to cut up – once he'd found the scissors.

It was all go, but by the time his day dream was over, he was knackered and as it was now eleven by the bedroom clock he decided to get up and visit the pub for lunch.

***

Success is a word, it's not a way of life.

As a cold grey dawn broke outside the warm doorway of Cayman Executive Finances, Big John, a burly homeless man, gathered his cardboard and meagre belongings. He knew a good thing when he found it and didn't want staff turning up and making a complaint that would cause his relocating. The night had passed with one interesting incident, a false alarm call to the fire brigade from the nearby hotel. John had a good relationship with the hotel staff, who would often find him suitable leftovers from the evening meals. He had shared a friendly chat and a cup of tea with the fire-fighters that night. Big John was a likeable, tee-total man and previously owned a smallholding business, which gave him an air of respectability. He couldn't cope any more with four walls, it was his freedom that kept him sane. Regardless of the weather, he took life in his stride and with a smile on his face. As he wandered with his few but useful possessions in the direction of the local park, he nodded a friendly hello to the early morning postman and received a cheery wave in reply. They had much in common, both out in rain or shine while most were still tucked up under their duvets.

An hour or so after John had left 'home' at the prestigious Cayman Executive Finances building, the silence was broken by the arrival of chief executive Clive 'wonder boy' Rothenchild. Roaring into his reserved parking space in his red Ferrari, he was ready to start work and kickass in the world of banking, a euphemism for shifting poor people's money into rich people's offshore bank accounts. Even with the windows closed, his new age 'rock a bully', music almost ruptured the eardrums of a passing stray dog. Clive made his way to the grand entrance, where he had to wait briefly for the caretaker to unlock. 'Good day sir, lovely morning now,' he welcomed with a smile. Clive stared in fury at the annoying cretin someone had obviously mistaken as suitably employable and ignored him. Clive took the lift, one floor up, and hoped his dim-witted secretary would be in early just as he'd texted, late last evening.

Clive entered his office, turned up the heating and took off his coat, briefly stopping to admire himself in one of several office mirrors. He sat at his desk, turned on his computer and drummed his fingers impatiently while it warmed up. It requested his personal password to continue.

He tapped them in slowly with one clumsy finger,

S H E E P, a £ sign and a smiley face.

His soulless and greedy eyes led his equally soulless and greedy mind to look out of the window and survey the land of peasants, all ready for fleecing. He snarled a few words at his secretary as she hurried in, looking flustered. 'Get your act together deary, I've got important friends visiting today. No mistakes, right? Smarten yourself up too, you look a mess, like you've been up all night.'

She forced a smile, looking after two small children and a sick husband was taking its toll on her and she'd had to pay through the nose to find a last-minute child minder so she could arrive early for work. She desperately needed to keep this job. 'Yes sir, of course sir. It's the mayor and head of chamber of commerce isn't it? I have everything organised for them, just as you asked.'

As she bustled off to prepare for his guests, he sneered under his breath, 'Dopey woman, no idea why I keep her.'

Let us now consider the successes of both these men.

One of them can find his way anywhere, in peace and calm, regardless of the weather, he is given food freely by those who care for him. He has no need of modern technology to get him though the day. He uses his mind creatively and is always willing to help others – he knows the meaning of gratitude and of empathy. He is rich in spirit and at peace with the world despite his various hardships. He lives in tune with the seasons. He is content with his cardboard box in the warm doorway of Cayman Buildings.

The other, has no friends except on social media, where pretence takes the place of honesty. He cannot find his way home without sat nav and is afraid to go out at night. No one makes him a dinner unless he pays for it. He must have holidays abroad in warm countries but no place he considers dirty. He has burglar alarms and cameras at his house. When not bragging on Facebook he watches TV. His success, if that is what you call it, comes from robbing old ladies of their pensions. (Perfectly legal, the small print does explain the risks.) He is despised by all who meet him. He has no soul. But his Ferrari tells the world he is successful.

What is your choice?
You'll hear your inner voice, but will you listen?
Of course not, you know better, don't you?

***

There's an app that does it all –
and it's yours today, for free !

The young lady was bored and so deep in thought about nothing; she stared lovingly at her mobile phone resting dormant on the coffee table in front of her. It was so clever, it was her companion, her confidante, it could play games too, it knew things she might never discover. Her eyes slowly drifted into a vacant fixation.

As she watched intently, mesmerised, a tiny hologram of a state-of-the-art salesman appeared floating just above her mobile phone.

"My goodness", she thought, "this is truly amazing, almost out of this world".

"That's nothing young lady, I shall now reveal to you something far greater than this mere toy. Relax and listen. I'm going to tell you about a translator which can detect even the slightest of accents and translate any language you choose to access. If you think that is good, wait till you realise that this device can tell when you are being told truth or lies and should you transgress yourself it will set off an alarm within you that encourages correction. The device has a built-in multipurpose calculator able to understand complex formulae as well as perform simple maths in an instant. It can what's more, be used to create stories, constructing meaningful sentences with correct spelling and grammar far beyond the capability of American spellcheck (a word which it doesn't even recognise itself). It contains a dictionary and a thesaurus geared to your own language and needs. The device is electronically connected within your body so you can locate words automatically without ever having to look at a key board, while doing so you can even carry out other functions, which we in the trade like to call multi-tasking. What do you think of it so far, young lady?"

"Oh, sorry, what was that? Oh yes, very, very good I definitely must buy one of these," she said without moving from her transfixed posture.

"Well let me tell you more, young lady. What I tell you now about the device all comes free, along with unlimited usage and no running costs or set up fees. It will continue to record memory for a lifetime and has an information retrieval system second to none; even finding files with no labels. It gives intelligent and instantaneous recall of events, places, people and even concepts connected to a bio feedback link that allows you to seemingly relive the sensations of those accessed memories. The memory function can also be used as a forward planner, reminding you of appointments, birthdays and the like. There is so much in this device that it would take more than a lifetime to explore, in fact it is fathomless. Do you want to know more?"

"Oh yes please", she said automatically, this all sounded too good to be true but something in the salesman's voice told her there was indeed a deep truth in what he was saying.

"Okay, young lady," he continued, "this device can automatically detect, analyse and distinguish body language, so revealing the true intention behind another's actions. It has an inbuilt warning system that runs completely independently of all other operations and activates through bio feedback to prepare the body for action. As a young person you might be also interested in the inbuilt health monitor. It can inform you when you are not in the best of health, about which foods are best for your body type, when you need rest and if a visit to a health professional is recommended."

There was a timeless pause of complete nothingness, akin to what the gurus might consider a highly prized state of deep meditation.

"Well enough of the serious stuff," the salesman continued, "what about leisure? Again, all for free and accessible almost at will is a virtual cinema where you can not only watch documentaries or complete fiction but can experience them just as if you really were there. The device allows you to interact with the characters, even change the story line and become different people within the show. The electronic bio feedback circuits allow you to experience heat, cold, happiness, danger, in fact all physical experiences. You will be able through the virtual cinema to run, climb and swim, everything will be as real. It is possible that great wisdoms will be yours during the experience. What is more the device is so clever that an entire epic of several hours will be shown in your virtual cinema in the blink of an eye, all in the comfort of your own home and in such vivid colours you'll wonder how it is possible. All for free, no questions asked, no data required to be stored by some unscrupulous person then stolen by someone else of an even greater malcontent… it will be just your experience alone. No passwords required and totally secure from any living hackers. Interested?"
"Oh yes, where can I obtain such a device, I need one of these for sure?" she said with a conviction tinged with anticipation.

"Let me ask you, what about this device kept your attention?" the salesman enquired, leaning forward and closer.

"Er, well, the clever way you advertise it with this holographic and interactive image I guess," she replied, not quite so sure, now that she was pressured to think for herself.

"Wrong, young lady, it's a figment of your imagination that created the interest, the device of which I spoke is in your mind; the only problem is that despite knowing it exists . . . you still refuse to use it!"

The salesman vanished instantly as the mobile's klaxon warned of an urgent incoming message, demanding a frenzied instant response, or else. Her hand instinctively reached out as though it too was excited by the irresistible call. It must be answered regardless of who was on the other end, or indeed what she was doing at the time.

It was a text from her friend, all about having just chipped a nail while opening the toilet door in the supermarket; our young lady replied on auto pilot, tapping in the complex codes without a glance at the screen. . .

"Hi Rebbeca, you'll nvr gueS w@ jst hapnd, I jstwatchd a holographic advert 4 an app dat dzabsolutel evryting. I'm jst goin on 2 Googl en C whr I cn buy 1."

Prediction: - they'll all be very sorry one day when they discover what they could have done with their life !

***

The Bank Holiday Shift.

"Smith! In here now," snarled the police chief inspector, who'd just found out that his only free days off this year were to be blighted by his wife's family visiting. The outlaws he called them, the mother-in–law being a cross between Maggie Thatcher, Lucrecia Borgia and Eva Braun, and they were coming to stay for the entire bank holiday weekend. He wasn't a happy bunny and sure as eggs is eggs, he was going to make his displeasure felt in the one place where he had some vestige of power remaining, and that wasn't at home!

"Don't sit down Smith, you're not stopping. I've swapped your shift around, so you are working on May Day Bank Holiday, you'll be working for CID and in plain clothes. You're to spend the day in the municipal park, stay till they close the gates at night. Apparently, there's a bunch of weirdos that hang about the kiddies play area, watch for them, gather any evidence and phone it through to CID . . . if you can ever find one on a bank holiday that is. Take your family with you, make it look good . . . we don't want you arrested as a weirdo, do we? You don't want to spend your bank holiday in a police cell eh? (While secretly thinking that might be a good way that he could avoid his own outlaws.) It certainly would be quieter than listening to his wife's mother, a widow now twice grieved by husbands that chose suicide before continued marriage. He knew what she'd go on about . . . her neighbour's cats for a start; he knew all about them, he'd heard it all before.

"But sir, with respect, it's my first . . . " Smith started to protest.

"Shut it Smith, do as you are ordered . . . and close the door on your way out," smirked the chief inspector who was beginning to feel better already.

"You are joking I hope!" screamed his normally kindly wife as he told her the news, "your only day off this year and we could have taken the children somewhere nice together, what are you like? I don't know why I married you, or am I married to that idiot chief inspector and the service?"

"Look dear, the wages pay the mortgage and buy our food, I can't get out of it. Why don't we all go together, you can do anything you like at the park, there's crazy golf, (she gave him a strange stare at this point) tennis courts, a café, in fact loads of things, you and the kids can go on everything you like and no quibbling over prices, I'll pay for it all, I'm on double time for a bank holiday," he assured her with as best a generous smile as he could muster.

His wife thought for a while, thinking about the kids playing several rounds of golf or tennis while she tried out the café's selection of cream cakes or read her book under a tree. "Okay, you're on, the park it is."

Bank holiday and they all walked to the park in the sunshine, it's one of the best days of the year and quite unusual for the traditional weather for a bank holiday. He handed out several coins to the two children, exacting from them a promise to spend it wisely and bring him the receipts as proof of their choice. The kids couldn't believe their luck, money in hand to spend as they chose and freedom to roam about the park without the nagging that parents like to call advice. Wonderful, a great day.

Meanwhile, on his rest day, the chief inspector was washing up at home, the dishwasher already full to the brim. He muttered to himself, 'it's like feeding the 5,000, except even Jesus couldn't put up with this lot.' The sound of his washing up on the dark side of the house was drowned out by wild cackling and snorting from the mother-out-law, almost certainly a joke at his expense.

The working day was going well, happy people all in the sunshine, not a sign of a weirdo among them, kids laughing at their tennis prowess or lack of it, a happy wife full of cream cakes and the special coffees that she had discovered in the cafe bar. Sure, he'd spent a lot but after all, it's only money!

Come the Wednesday it was back in uniform at the station, a bright, tanned and cheerful constable knocked on the door of a bleary eyed and wan looking chief inspector. "Come in," said a defeated sounding voice, "Come in."

"Good morning sir, I hope you had a good holiday. Nothing to report about weirdos in the park sir, all clear. Can you just approve my expenses claim that CID told me to submit sir?" he asked, handing over a long form with countless receipts attached, some of them for double ice creams with chocolate flakes and one or two at the back with coffee and baileys overwritten with 'refreshments'.

The chief inspector, now a broken man, didn't even glance at the expenses form but scribbled his name weakly in the approved place. Without looking up he slid the paper back across his desk, "anything else I can do for you Smith?"

"Oh yes sir, can you put my name down for the next bank holiday shift."

***

The Burial.

'What have you boys been burying in my garden,' wheezed Granny Smith, peering into the darkness and leaning on her frame.

'Give it a rest Gran, it's nothing to bother your old brain about, you never go down the far end of your garden anyway?' Came a terse and disrespectful reply from Nathan, her 30-year-old grandson. Well her daughter said he was, but he was nothing like any of her other family.

'That may be my boy, but what have you buried?'

'It's only my girlfriend's cat Gran, it needed some big vet bills, so I sorted it for her, that's all,' Nathan smirked in the half darkness. He knew she would believe that of him and it would stop her from having someone dig it up and shame would stop her talking about it to her neighbours. He was on a winner with this.

Granny Smith, first name Rosie, was a good woman and one who had already endured a hard life. Her father had been crippled fighting for his country but still turned in an honest day's work up until his heart attack. Her mother was clever, kindly and pretty too, and could have had a much different life if it wasn't for the sacrifices she had made for her children. Good people all, hardworking but always living in simple, some would say, primitive conditions. Rosie Smith now 82 lived in a small council house, one of the few remaining. She had heating and an indoor toilet – sheer luxury compared to her parent's old home, and she was grateful. Mind you, she too had worked most of her life and only ever bought what she could afford, unlike many younger folks of today, who already spend the pension they have yet to earn.

Nathan was an odd kettle of fish; he scrounged or stole what he could with never a thought for others. He did lots of work for cash in hand so as not to pay tax and lived for free on benefits. To fiddle himself a mobility car, perhaps a BMW, was one of his greatest dreams.

All very good reasons why he couldn't be caught with the £12 thousand pounds in new £10 notes that he'd buried in his Gran's garden. Give it a couple more months and he could safely dig it up again, then he could enjoy the life he deserved.

As for his Gran, he partly wished her dead, I mean that's why young people must pay taxes, to look after these old useless people who were a drain on the country's resources. He was paying for them all to sit around doing nothing while he went without.

Nathan thought on this a lot. Take his silly old Gran for instance, he later heard that the local day care centre she went to once a week had been gifted a load of money so they could all have a weekend at the seaside. Disgusting waste of money being spent on old people, why wasn't someone paying for him to go to the seaside?

Then the night of nights eventually arrived for Nathan to return and dig up his well-earned treasure. Granny Rosie Smith watched from the comfort of an upstairs window with the room lights switched off.

'He's in for a bit of a wakeup call that boy,' she thought to herself, as a frenzied, almost rabid, Nathan searched one hole after another, again and again in mortified disbelief.

Granny Smith was a lot stronger than she looked.

***

The Card at Christmas.

When the card arrived, I realised it was still telling a story that rings true today.

The unmarried mother is given free accommodation, the unknown father is absent, but she has taken up with another, a traveller, a man who sells his skills for money. When the kindly landlord is out of the way, she moves her boyfriend in and he in turn brings in some rich people, who say they have travelled from afar with gifts. Hoping for a new TV or a laptop he doesn't hesitate. There's not a lot of room in the new pad because they've also brought their pet donkey with them, despite it clearly defying and defiling house rules.

They're all hungry and the boyfriend says, 'God, I could murder a turkey, I'm starving.' As luck would have it, the landlord had foolishly thought his lambs would be safe in the barn and so it wasn't too long before a fire was lit and mutton kebabs the order of the day. The mother said, 'you'll have to tell the landlord that it was some people hanging about outside what must have nicked them, sort of hell's angels they was, tell him. Pass another kebab and chuck another log on the fire … we're not paying for any of it.'

It should be no surprise that the child eventually grew up with an anti-society attitude. A dysfunctional adult, he railed against the laws of the land and became a thorn in the side of the then legitimate Roman government. Funny, isn't it, they always blame the parents and their upbringing for their own demise?

All allegedly of course.

***

The Dinner Party.

It was a special day for the County's unofficial food guide group. They'd mostly met via face-book and trip advisor, where they had a reputation for the most savage and vociferous honesty about the qualities of the various pubs they invaded, I mean visited. Today there were only fourteen of them, should be easy enough for the pub, pah, pub, it had the nerve to call itself an Inn and it had changed names a few times too. Remember Windscale? They changed their name too. Most of the members had partners of varying attachments, seemed more respectable that way and who knows they might get lucky. The men were predominantly either office workers retired on incompetence grounds or failed Masonic applicants both of which promoted a desire for revenge and to re-establish their sense of deserved power of which they had been so unjustly robbed. Some of the women used to work the counters of Woolworths before it closed down. Anyway, they arrived and pulled into the car park, pompously parking with little consideration for others but spread out to allow an easy and thoughtless swing of their own car doors into unobstructed space. They started to make notes as they walked towards the main road which separated them from their victim . . . the affable and kindly Landlord of the Blue Ball.

'Car park untidy; needs fresh gravel.' 'Poor view of Church, trees in way.'
'Don't like the colour of the walls.' 'Needs a woodshed … and not on the main road.' 'Motorcycle came by too quick.' 'Weather inclement, too windy and cold, looks like it rains here.' 'Hill too steep.' The Inn was already down to a two star and they hadn't opened the front door yet.

Inside, the happy staff were busying themselves in preparation for their famous Sunday lunches. The landlord noticed the hotel entrance door was ajar, left the bar and went to close it, it seemed stuck, then he realised it was being held by a plump little woman smelling of lavender and possibly something like onions. He stepped back to allow the customers through, some did, and he retreated to the bar where he could best be of service. About four actually came that way into the bar area. While the plump one held the hotel entrance door open to the moorland weather and peered into what must have seemed like mist or darkness to her squinting eyes, the remainder of the group entered by the proper Inn door and stood in a mess of people that prevented the it being opened by anyone else. Still, who cares, they were all accounted for. Still, the plump one, who must have had a managerial position in Woolworths, stared out into the cold, a light drizzle having made the glass of her spectacles look like bathroom glazing.

The chair of the group, a struck off solicitor, but that's a secret, stepped forward to the bar, peering from a distance into the welcoming eyes of the landlord. (He would have stood closer, but rotundness prevented him.) 'You'll be expecting us, we booked lunches for eight but there are fourteen of us, I'm sure you won't mind, it looks like you could do with some decent custom,' he said looking around the room at a tall bald chap with a red wine and roast dinner, he shifted the obvious plumb in his mouth and spoke again, 'right my good man, show us your best tables.'

'Oh no, no, they won't do, they really won't, what about over there, you can move those tables around so we can all sit together, there's a good little man.'

The landlord was a fair but firm man but none the less he decided to oblige the group this once. With some assistance from his likeable and hardworking staff pulled from other tasks, he rearranged the tables.

'We'll order from here,' shouted a rather uncouth woman who was obviously with the rotund ex solicitor and at one time probably loosely employed on the Woolworths sweets counter until being dismissed for sucking the chocolate off the Brazils.

The landlord thought for a moment then agreed; as, to be honest, it would be better if they stayed away from the bar. 'I'll be back in a moment,' he said bumping into the wet plump one who had only just realised she was on her own at the door.

More notes were made, furious scribblings, in more than one sense of the word; 'Very poor table layout, no thought for decent sized parties,' 'Rather draughty, felt like a door was open somewhere, thoughtless,' 'ghastly décor and there was a hole in the carpet too,' 'horrible black curly haired dog tried to get past me into the pub, had to use my foot to keep it out, obviously some half-baked nutter's dog,' 'we seem to be waiting a long time for service, don't they know who we are?'

The plump one threw her wet coat over a piece of polished furniture; it shouldn't matter as it all looked like it came from Oxfam anyway. She managed to squeeze herself into an empty chair near one corner.

'Where's the landlord?' demanded the ex-solicitor.
'He's busy with some other customers at the moment, can I take your orders for drinks please, if you are ready,' smiled the young barmaid.
'Just tap water for me,' 'Make that three,' 'no, four'. 'A bottle of Red and nothing from South America or Eastern

Europe if you don't mind.' 'a babysham,' 'a J2O, what flavours have you got? No, I don't like those, make it a lager instead.' Make that five tap waters,' 'I'll change the lager for a guiness, is it extra cold?' 'A gin and tonic … not the cheap tonic, if you only have that I'll have a rum and coke, but not diet coke, if you only have that I'll have a pernod and blackcurrant.' 'two local beers here, and three white wines, as long as they're not warm or come from Germany.' 'scotch on the rocks here, and none of that imported crap.'

There you go dear and have one on us,' said the ex solicitor, eyes like hands running over her body.

'Thank you kindly sir but I'm fine, I'll take your order through and return to take your food orders,' with that she turned and left … even thought about keeping on walking … out the door and all the way home, but she didn't.

'Ah, waiter, at last some service,' pomped the ringleader of the gang to the landlord, who had saved his young barmaid from the maddening crowd and put his own life and reputation on the line instead.

The landlord ignored any comments, smiled and asked if they were ready to order. Three people spoke at once and continued to do so until they had finished. He picked up odd words from each person, 'no lobster on menu,' 'meat pie homemade,' 'just a salad with side order chips', 'what's in gravy,' etc.

'Okay, let's start again, from this end, one at a time please.'

The landlord's comments were greeted with looks of thunder, it reminded them of when they were at work, they'd been treated just the same, no respect for their own brilliant offerings. However, they complied . . . their day would come as sure as Satan lives in hell.

'Roast dinner, pork but only if the pig died happily, two yorkshires and extra roast potatoes, and none of that burnt pig fat and skin you try and fob off as crackling.' One down thirteen to go, the pub would be closing before he can sort this lot out.

'Next.'

'Isn't there a specials board I can look at, I don't much fancy your printed menu, oh, hang on, yes, I see now, er . . . . . er . . . . . what do you think, shall I have the baked potato with cheese, . . . er or perhaps tuna, . . . yes that's it tuna baked potato. No changed my mind I'll have the cheese. But only if it's French cheddar.' She was previously employed in a police control room . . . until her dithering caused such protests from all ranks that she was retired on ill health and a huge pension, of which she was careful in spending . . . very careful.

'Next please.'

'Six roast dinners at this end, all beef.'

At last a sensible order. But . . .

'No parsnip on two of them Peas instead of cauliflower on one, and no gravy on two of them, are they new or old potatoes? Doesn't matter, no potatoes on one.'

The order was interrupted by a thin bespectacled man jumping up and shouting a muffled expletive of unknown origin. The cause of his agitation slowly straightened up in her chair . . . the plump one had inadvertently interfered with his groin as she'd groped about under the table for her handbag. Totally oblivious of her actions and their effect, she began to order her dinner, 'vegan roast for me dear,' she said squinting at the boar's head wall trophy having mistaken it for the waiter.

The landlord simply recorded 'veggie dinner,' it occurred to him that one with awareness such as hers must have disabled the connection between taste buds and brain by now.

'Next,'

'Have you taken my order yet?' enquired a confused and strangely dressed lady in the middle, it also looked like she was confused while finding clothes for her day out. She couldn't remember what day out and indeed, looking around the table, she wasn't quite sure who half the people were . . . 'must be someone's birthday,' she thought.

'No madam, what would you like?' smiled the rapidly tiring landlord.

'Don't you have any menus dear?' she responded on the assumption that the waitress was very tall for a woman and poor girl was nearly bald.

'That's a menu you are holding madam, why don't I recommend something or perhaps one of your friends will help.'

They all knew better and either stared out of the window or a very interesting crack in the plaster. 'The roast dinners are good madam, perhaps a small portion would suit,' the landlord held his pen at the ready.

'Can't you get on with it man, I'm waiting for my dinner, must have ordered it an hour ago by now, and make sure your half portion for Miss Memory here isn't charged at full price. We're pensioners you know. Not made of money like some,' growled the ex-solicitor peering intently and accusingly under his eyebrows. God he'd like to see this man in a dock in front of him. . . there'd be no slap dash dilly dally faffing about then.

  As the landlord turned towards the kitchen, staring at his scribbled note, even more furious scribbling was going on behind him from the pub guide contingent. He thought he heard, 'I think I'll change my mind . . . er. . . .'

but he pretended he hadn't heard. 'They probably won't remember what they ordered anyway,' he mumbled, not even sure if he'd actually got all fourteen of the little darling's orders.

Furious notes from the group, with conferring, now the idiot had gone.
'Waitress unsuitable, too tall, bald and with a deep voice . . . puts you off your dinner,' Waiter completely confused about what he has or hasn't got on the menu.' 'Off putting whiskered dark-haired bloke continually staring at me', wrote the plump one mistaking the boar's head trophy for a man and the tablecloth for her notebook. 'The presence of dogs can be off putting when they search for crumbs under the table,' 'the presence of dogs touching your legs under the table was a welcome change from the usual pub visits,' (from a lady in her 50's who had joined hoping to meet her soul mate, however it would be more likely to meet a cell mate with this bunch). 'Ceiling's too low, not enough light,' 'ceilings too high, too bright, needs more subtle romantic lighting,' 'not enough attention to when a man's glass is empty, should be shot,' (guess who.)

It all went very well, and their comments are available on trip advisor.

The landlord they say is on holiday . . . they won't say where, until the doctor says he can come home.

***

Lent losses.

It was the warm spring of 2010, Ben shouted down the stairs, 'it's a funeral for God's sake, where's my old suit?'

There was a silence from below, a silence laden with palpable guilt and there was no escaping it. 'Oh Benjamin, I remember now, I mean you hadn't worn that old suit for years . . .' she was curtly interrupted, 'of course not, nobody's bloody died for years, where the hell is it?' Ben's wife, Sarah, knew it was pointless this time to argue . . . she was guilty. 'I lent it to Mrs Sopworthy around the corner . .'

Ben interrupted again, with incredulity, 'what the hell does that little plump woman want with a man's suit for god's sake?' (God and Hell seemed to be having a special outing today.)

Sarah wanted to say, 'don't be so stupid,' but thought better of it, 'It was to lend to her uncle who was going to a funeral, he wanted to look respectful at the ceremony, surely you can see that dear?'

There was a silence as Ben sat on the end of the bed in his underpants and thought deeply about the poignancy of the last sentence. Perhaps he could find something else to wear, if his wife hadn't lent it all out.

Ben didn't go in the end as he had developed a migraine. Sarah thought it best to leave him in peace and went shopping; there were some nice shoes in a sale in town.

Two hours later, Sarah was showing off two new pairs of shoes to her WI friends in Maxim's Bistro. Okay it was a little expensive in there, but they had really nice curtains and comfy chairs. The food wasn't that good either but was beautifully presented . . . that sort of thing made all the difference.

One of the other ladies commented on a pair of the shoes, 'Oh, aren't they lovely, I had a pair like that once, seeing them here reminded me of them. Not seen them for years, Mrs Sopworthy borrowed them for a film premier she said she was invited to attend. I'd forgotten about them until now.'

Another lady chipped in, 'Is that the little plump lady that lives near Sarah? She borrowed our lawn mower last November. I remember her saying theirs was in for service and the gardener needed a last cut before winter. My old man, Bob, is furious about it, he went to the shed to get it out as the grass has begun to grow again and of course it wasn't there. I hardly dare tell him what I'd done but as he was about to phone the police and report a burglary I had to confess.'

Their cream cakes and coffee, in a really fancy but tiny, silver pot, arrived. As their eyes surveyed the cakes with the eyes of scavenging hyenas, Mrs Blinkingsworth–Smythe assured them that all would be well. Why? She had herself entrusted Mrs Sopworthy with a ruby necklace that had been handed down for centuries in her husband's family. 'Now I wouldn't have done that if she wasn't entirely trustworthy. It was last year for a Palace garden party, or her husband getting an MBE or something. I must ask her for it back. Does anyone know her address?'

'I think the lady in question has moved madam,' said a hovering waiter, 'she came into some money and went upmarket to Kingston or somewhere near. We were surprised that coming into so much money, she didn't settle her bills before leaving. And the manageress had kindly lent her a lovely coat to walk home in one really cold night too.'

The pretty waitress joined in, 'You must mean Joan, Joan Sopworthy, used to live near my Gran and made her living at car boot sales and through E Bay. My Gran said she did very well out of it too, except was never for some reason able to sell the Victorian table lamp Gran handed over for her to sell. Any way she's gone now, and her house sold for over three hundred thousand they say. More coffee anyone?'

Sarah wondered if she might find a cheap suit in the sales – just in case someone else was to die in the near future.

***

The man who wouldn't take the monkey home.
The cautionary, allegedly true story about immense personal success gained through conscious and intentional neglect of another's legitimate needs.
Names changed to protect. . . er. . . me mostly !

We'll call him Brutus Maximus for the sake of argument. His subordinate will be played by me. We both worked in the same fictitious training department for a local authority fire service, a hierarchical organisation which requires employees to follow orders and observe the chain of command, regardless of circumstance. Even word, act or demeanour could constitute punishable offences.

Long before I was enlightened about the 'no monkey' policy, which Brutus had implemented starting at his office door, I witnessed one or two other self-interested behaviours. For example, the department had a limited number of drill books for students and reference. On special days, when practical examinations were held for promotion exams, each examining officer was given one to use (The applicants were expected to possess detailed knowledge without the aid of such book – in order to rise to the level where they too could forget the contents.) My job was to issue these few books and ensure their safe return for others to use. Brutus lost his and when I explained he had already been issued with one, he leapt about screaming, 'get me another one then.' Orders is orders as they say and he duly had his second book.

Prior to his unexpected (by the rest of us anyway) promotion to head of department, Brutus would always join in a practical day out exercise with officer students. It involved a pleasant day's walk in the countryside watching other people struggle with initiative tasks and always culminated in beer and sandwiches on a small remote riverbank. Once Brutus was head of department, he could no longer avail himself of such pleasures and to make sure nobody else did, he scrapped that exercise from the course.

One of the tests for recruits into the service was a dexterity test and on this occasion, it was a hacksaw which had been dismantled and had to be reassembled by the student in a given and reasonable time . . . preferably without breaking or losing any bits. For some reason, known only to him, Brutus (with power of life or death over any application) was prepared to pass a particular applicant on a hacksaw that had been reconstructed, (you might prefer the description completely redesigned) with the blade back to front and upside down and the locator bolt protruding dangerously from the wrong side. Brutus must have sensed our collective horror associated with employing someone with such dubious skills in an essentially practical lifesaving job and changed his mind. Perhaps the chap was a relative, or perhaps Brutus was just feeling peculiarly benevolent, perhaps somewhere along the line a monkey was waiting.

One more example before I explain about the monkey reference. I was tasked with writing behavioural objectives for the service training programme (incidentally, never implemented despite a year's work). Sometimes he would 'correct' the objectives in red pen. When I could see that Brutus was misguided, I simply had the original retyped and submitted. How odd that it received approval next time. Was wielding the red pen just an illustration of power without logic? The behavioural objectives always started off with something like –'At the end of this session the student should be able to do this or that'. Brutus thought this was wrong and ordered me to change 'should' to 'will'. I tried to explain that there is no guarantee that a student *will* succeed only that given favourable opportunity they *should* succeed. Brutus told me quite clearly, 'you *should* write *will*.' I said 'exactly', rested my case and we wrote '*should*,' with his reluctant approval.

Okay, monkeys. Many a time I would visit the office, which Brutus commanded in omnipotent solitude, with some problem that the department was experiencing. For example; 'The breathing apparatus course at the weekend doesn't have enough staff for safety.' Foolishly expecting him to look at the staff rota and transfer someone to assist.

His answer, 'I'll leave it with you, do what you can, perhaps someone on the fire station can help.'

Such answers were never very helpful and often stressful; we were burdened with great responsibility and no power to carry it out. Brutus had the power but constantly declined the responsibility. Remember, we could not complain, for the highly disciplined chain of command leads through the problem himself.

Then one day he confided, in fact he lent me his copy of the article to read, all about avoiding problems – for you anyway. I've no idea what idiot (I'm not afraid) wrote it. The methodology was to see all problems as monkeys. When approached by a member of staff bringing a problem, visualise it as a monkey. Under no circumstances let the staff member leave your office without taking the monkey away with them. If you get stuck with the monkey you have to take it home at night, feed it the next morning and drive it back to work where it will sit on your desk all day annoying you before you drive it home for dinner. There was no sign on the door that warned, 'No problems - no monkeys past this point.' It was a secret which eventually led him to two more prestigious promotions culminating in an office at headquarters where his 'no problem' approach must have engendered an ignorant admiration of him. I went there once, after he'd denied ever receiving important documents sent six months previous – his desk was empty, polished shiny and empty . . . all the monkeys living somewhere else I guess, or retired on ill health.

Conscious and selective negligence can lead to great rewards for those who neither give nor take a monkey's . . .

It was never my way, I had enough monkeys to fill a zoo, and I've just released one into the wild. If you find it, do make sure it's okay, won't you?

***

I may be empty now but . .
it wasn't always that way.
About an old house.

Once upon a time, boisterous children in ungainly play ran along my hallway, their thudding footfalls reverberating through my very foundations. The unmistakable smell of half cooked mutton wafted from my kitchen and through the half-closed doors to my lounge where wood smoke haze idly mingled with tobacco. Guests beat at the entrance porch, begging leave to come in and be entertained, their rain-soaked coats finding sanctuary in my vestibule. Beer and wine slopped its inebriated way across my floorboards, leaving graffiti stain memories of past wild parties. Wellington boots stood their skeletal sentry by the back door, still caked in mud from their daily incursions into the vegetable patch. At night, all would be mouse quiet but for the crackle of the unguarded fire, a dog that smelled of cow dung sniffing and scratching by the bins and the steady, near musical snoring from the man of the house . . . and his wife. Occasionally my timbers creaked, bringing his wife instantly bolt upright and wide awake with fear and him awake too by reason of his wife's well practised elbow. I too kept still and listened with them. There was nothing more to hear and soon they played out their nocturnal opera again. Some years later, the family of humans found a better house and abandoned me to the ravages of approaching winter and though I may be empty now. . . it's not in a way you might suppose.

I am at peace with the world, fresh air courses freely through every nook and cranny and sunshine liberally enters without the barrier of curtains to deny the coming of day or night. Nature herself shelters beneath my roof. The previous tenants left without a thank you, their parting gift, a heap of rubbish in the kitchen and a mildewed sheep skin rug in the vestibule. They could not put up with taking the smell with them and left it for us, but it wasn't so long before it dried out and provided comfortable bedding and nesting material for lots of new and grateful families. A family of rats who had patiently waited years for a new home moved in and soon had all the rubbish taken under the floorboards and recycled into a spacious rodent hotel.

Pointing the finger of despondency and saying, 'what a shame it is empty,' you fail to see we are full, full to the brim with space, nature, freedom. A home to all that seek an open door or window, a place for birds to nest and not be condemned, a sanctuary in the truest sense of the word, empty only to eyes that cannot see. No loneliness abides here; summer roosting bats enjoy their own company in the safety of the rafters, while the winter sheltering owl enjoys its solitude in relative warmth. Rabbits, moles and shrews fulfil their rightful place in nature's kaleidoscope and the vegetable garden matures under Persephone's footsteps. There's a place for each and each is in its place; indeed, ours is a happy, happy world.

We love the sound of rain on the roof and the howl of wind in the eaves as we also love the muted hush of fog and snow, we welcome with open hearts the patter of pads on our wooden boards but we share that one awful fear – the sound of wheels on gravel.

***

The meeting

The number 21A bus drew abruptly to a halt, two elderly ladies slowly met at the open door, one to dismount and one to board. However, as they both stood on the sun warmed pavement their eyes met briefly just long enough to spark some distant recognition. . . surely, they knew each other. Their pupils had briefly dilated as one peered through her rose tinted glasses and the other over the top of her bifocals, triggering a reminiscence response in their brains; Brains that were now racing overtime to remember who the other was, before being beaten to it.
The bus driver, already running late, closed the doors and left.

Neither of them noticed its going, they had stuff to talk about. Each knew they must ask questions until a suitable clue emerged in the quest to identify their friendly stranger.

Lovely to see you again, how long has it been? Came the smile from behind the Rose tinted specs.

Must be ages now, I can't remember. How have you been keeping?

Not so bad since catching a bout of dengue in South Africa . . . a rather difficult time.

Oh, how lovely, that's some sort of antelope, isn't it? Was it a difficult place to be for you there?

Not so much for me, but Bob being mauled to death by baboon troupe was quite shocking to watch. I have it on video, I'll show you one day.

I don't remember your husband's name, was it Robert then?

Oh God no, Clarence was serving six years in the scrubs for embezzlement at that time. Don't you remember, Bob was my miniature poodle, he died defending my handbag after a baboon stole it for the contents.

Can't say as I remember him now. Tell me, do you still live in the old place?

Yes, and you?

How are the children? All grown up I suppose now.

David is doing really well after dropping out of school with no qualifications and is now manager of a high-class dancing studio in Thailand. You'll remember Mavis of course; she was killed in a hot air balloon accident in Bolivia. How is your family these days?

Both mum and dad are passed away now and my civil partner Imogen left me. It was heart breaking because she took custody of Cyril and moved to Cuba.

Oh, how sad for you, does Cyril keep in touch?

Oh, poor Cyril, no, being a Burmese long haired cat, he can't write. But I bet he'd love to, all the same. I still keep tins of the luxury cat food, Fishycrap, in my cupboard, just in case he makes his way home on his own. Have you any pets now?

Not anymore. Since my neighbour attacked and ate another resident's gerbils, all pets are banned at the home. But we do still feed the pigeons in the park.

Oh, which park is that then?

The one we used to play in as children, you know, the one with the swings. By the way, did you go to the same school as Miriam Tufty?

No, I don't think so, did you?

No, but I saw in the local paper she died recently, quite suddenly.

Shame, heart attack?

Run over by a bus it said. Talking of buses, here comes your bus now. I suppose I must be getting home myself. Lovely to see you again, you really must pop by for a coffee some day and we can chat about old times. If you remind me, I'll dig out the video of Bob with the baboons, the scenery is stunning.

The lady with rose tinted specs climbed aboard the 21A and continued a journey she didn't want, while the lady with the bifocals, squinted after the disappearing bus before remembering she should have been on it.

Still, next time she meets her dear old friend, they will have lots to talk about.

Whoever she was . . .

***

The misery of increasing poverty in
a first world country.

(Based on a real local radio interview with the much
vaunted and feared Spanish human rights campaigner,
Mona Del Mucho.)
Names have been changed to protect the guilty and the
characters of this story bear no resemblance to anyone
living or dead.
The **interviewer is the Italian born investigative journalist
Mia Turner**, winner of the internationally acclaimed
Nosebag of the Year Award 2016.
The **interviewee is an anti government, pro death penalty,
traditional benefits claimant** since birth and campaigner
for fairer social funds distribution. Ms Elsie Snoot.

'So, may I call you Elsie, Ms Snoot? I understand
that you are unhappy with the new government's plans to
make a fair difference between those who work for a living
and those who do not?'

'That's alright for you to say, you've got yourself some
fancy job with loads of money, daddy probably paid for
your private school and you have no idea of the starving
under privileged and uneducated life of the abandoned
lower classes. We too have rights you know.'

A little taken aback by this aggressive attitude, Mia decided
not to argue about her own impoverished background or
the hard work she'd put in to obtain qualifications, whilst
still working a couple of part time jobs to pay her own way
in life. 'So, did you have trouble with transport attending
the studio, Elsie?'

'No, I came in my own car. Parking is easy with the blue badge. . . I'm on the double yellows outside the front entrance.'

Mia shuddered at the thought, she had fought long and hard to be granted a parking space at the studios and for which she paid £475 a year to enjoy the privilege. 'I suppose you can only afford a small vehicle on your benefits, what do you drive?'

'It's a 4x4 BMW, latest model, only had it replaced last week for a new one. I'm entitled to a free car every three years on the mobility scheme. Just have to stick some fuel in it which I make up for by charging friends for lifts into town . . . they don't mind because I can park right outside whatever shops they want.'

Mia was beginning to dislike this woman in front of her, but she must remain politically correct and impartial, it was her job. Mia thought briefly about her own ten year old car sitting in her expensive parking spot. She knew it would need new tyres and a service soon. . . more outlay from her meagre average salary. 'Wouldn't you be better off with a different car?'

'Well I did think about a Jaguar at one time, but the BM has a bigger boot and is slightly shorter. My council house has been highly modified and the double garage is suited to the BM now.'

'I was thinking you might be better off with a much smaller, more economical car Elsie.'

'God no. I need one this big for visits to the food banks and other things.'

'What on earth other things require such a big car Elsie?'

'Well, twice a week I take my son, he still lives with me as part of his bail conditions, to his AA meetings and occasionally drive him to Wandsworth, Dartmoor or Bedford prisons to visit his friends. He's good boy really, just been let down by the government and society. Oh, and once a year I take some friends on holiday to Wales. Lovely place, Snowdonia. Have you been?'

No. Mia had not bloody been to bloody Snowdonia, she had to work for a living, she worked shifts at the studio and was on call for urgent news interviews and none of them in bloody Snowdonia. 'No Elsie I've not had that pleasure yet, perhaps one day I will. So, you share your house with your son then Elsie. Is that a bit crowded in your little council house? Is it a flat you have?'

'I should cocoa, it's a four-bed detached. Mind you, the garden is a nuisance but luckily it is done for me by the council . . . after all it is their garden, they should keep it tidy, shouldn't they? I mean what do we pay our rates for?'

Mia considered her own shabby and expensive one bedroom flat she shared with a friend.
Mia wondered what it would be like to have a garden . . . her mind drifted gently away. A curt instruction in her earpiece from the studio manager brought her to her senses.

'I don't suppose you have time for hobbies or social events, so how do you spend your days?'

'You never said a truer word Miss Turner, what with running the boy out on errands in the evening, he's always getting phone calls to visit a friend in town, funny thing is, he only spends a couple of minutes with them then wants to go home again. Strange, but he's a good boy. Running my neighbours to the Bingo . . . I usually stop for a few rounds myself. Makes a change from the big TV with surround sound, gives me a break from housework too, anyway, that which the daily carers haven't done. And lately I've been up to the eyeballs with my campaign against the new government assessments on benefits. Like the Spanish Inquisition it is and all to rob me of my rights as an upstanding citizen. Good job we have the European courts of Justice on our side, that's what I say.'

Mia wondered what else she might say. This woman was a freeloading, lazy, arrogant, scrounging bigot with a far better lifestyle and unconditional income to which Mia herself could ever aspire.
'Well thank you so much for talking to us about poverty in modern Britain. That was Ms Elsie Snoot giving us the low down on her suffering as a result of new government attacks on the poor.
'I'm Mia Turner for Real Lives Radio here in the Midlands. Have a lovely day and thank you for listening.'

Before they went off air, the last broadcast to be heard was Elsie Snoot asking for her fee in cash as she didn't want some greedy taxman stealing it off her.

The Party.

Ever been to one? It was an old school reunion party, held in one of the function rooms of the past-its-prime Granville Hotel. A group of once lithe and naively active pupils had been enticed together for old time's sake. Now, they're in their sixties with all the evidence of some disturbing decades on full display. Many were there out of curiosity – mostly about how well they had done compared with others from what had been a quite peculiar secondary school; closer to a mental institution than an educational establishment. There were those who did not attend, some having emigrated on welfare benefits to the Costa Much or Lands-of-grotty, one was in Broadmoor and others had passed beyond the grave. Three suicides, one murder, two liver failures and a missing-at-sea, all had places on the roll of honour.

Anyway, Barbara was determined to have a good time. As long as she retained most of her marbles, her own teeth and a driving licence; no free dinner was to be scoffed at.

Out of the twenty or so guests, there was just one boy she recognised and that was only because his father had owned the sweet shop and his son Robert had grown up looking just like him, bald, affable and plump. 'Know anyone else, Bobby?' Barbara asked, squinting short sighted eyes over her spectacles.

'Yes. Remember the pretty girl, Becky, who left school to become a gymnast? Well, see the dumpy, miserable woman with the bald patch, wearing a cardigan and glasses, the one with the wicker handbag? That's her.'

Barbara nodded an acknowledgement, even if she couldn't quite see her old classmate across the room. 'There's a really odd man here Bobby - look – there he is. The one with the Mac still on. I spoke with him earlier. I'm wondering if his name is Roger, but don't remember anyone in our class by that name.'

'What makes you think that then Barbara?'

'Well, I asked him if he remembered the school mascot . . . you remember the goat? Guess what he said . . . "Roger that willco," he said. In fact, he became quite excited about any animals I mentioned. He hardly said a word beyond, "Roger that." How odd can that be?'

'I don't think he's one of ours Barbara. He's probably from another group in the hotel. We did get this room very cheaply, provided we booked for today. Please excuse me a moment, I think that old chap asleep in the wheelchair might be our old maths teacher. Must go and wake him up and ask him about Pythagoras just for fun.'

Bobby left Barbara wracking her brains to remember any foreign boy in the class called Pythagoras. Perhaps more of her marbles had slipped down the back of her cerebral sofa than she realised.

Just as Barbara was about to pop a few sandwiches and cakes into her handbag for later, a hand slapped her on the back and a stranger's female voice bellowed, 'Myrtle dear, how are you? It's been ages.'

Barbara held her shoulder wondering if it was dislocated. The little woman behind her had the strength of ten men. 'I'm so sorry, you have the wrong person. My name is Barbara. Do I know you?'

'Of course you do, you silly billy Brenda. We worked together at the Seaman's Mission café, remember? You had an affair with that Russian captain . . . and his crew.'

Barbara's mind was in a spin. This woman was so certain she did know her. In fact, much more certain than Barbara thought she didn't.

'Did you go to Barlinney Secondary school then?' asked Barbara, trying to put pieces of distant jigsaw memory to use.

The little lady slapped Barbara's shoulder again, doing her a favour as it seemed to put the joint back in place. 'My dear Bridget, of course I did. My father was headmaster. He got the George Cross for working there you know.'

'Oh, I thought we had a headmistress, a big woman, dark curly hair, broad shoulders.'

'That's him Beverly. My, you have a good memory.'

A man's burly, authoritative voice interrupted them just as Barbara was on the edge of insanity and wondering if she was ever who she thought she was.

The large man took an arm lock on the little woman and apologised to Barbara. 'So sorry, Mavis is on a care in the community outing and gave us the slip. I hope she didn't disturb you too much.'

As Barbara returned to the cake table, she could hear Mavis being forcibly led away, still screaming, 'Wait, wait, I haven't asked Beatrice about the bike sheds yet. . .'

All eyes in the room turned to stare at the lady near the cake table with an open handbag. A murmur grew as they wondered who the hell she was.

***

The Priest and the Villain

'Even more letters for censoring Guv'ner,' said the prison officer, placing a second paper bundle on the mahogany desk.

"Er, thank you Williams, that will be all I think,' replied Hugh Wilberforce OBE, twenty years governor of Gragsville high security prison. His mind was still taken by two letters he'd just read, one coming in and one going out. He knew both correspondents personally. Firstly, Hatchet McGraw, twelve years for murder and a previous hit man for the notorious 'Instow gang'; secondly, Father James, retired Chaplin. They must have met in prison, for here they were, writing to each other. The Guv'ner picked up the letters thoughtfully and read them slowly a second time.

'I am pleased you felt able to write to me after such a serious setback in what could have been such a happy and prosperous life. You ask how I coped with the celibacy, and isolation in a world of non-believers. You'll know as much as me about being alone, no wife, no family; Long days running into long years of servitude. I give you my honest advice, seek peace with those around you, be on good terms with all and if nothing else, eliminate judgement. Explore meditation, there are books in the library and the prison chapel is a quiet place with few visitors . . . except for the odd drug deal. Most prisoners will be in the gym building bodies to protect themselves from others. My advice is to meditate spiritually and protect yourself from a hell of your own making.'

The Governor's attention turned to the letter he still held in his other hand:-

'I wrote to you three weeks ago and worry that you have chosen not to reply, having found my crimes too abhorrent to want further contact. I had hoped we had built a relationship and that we could share each other's troubles. I know the old prison saying, 'a friend in need . . . is a pain in the neck,' but I am in need of the advice of experience. Since being sentenced I have struggled to come to terms with my new surroundings.

There are some not so nice people in here and I remain afraid except for when in solitary. Tell me; I beg of you; how can I cope with these horrors?

Yours sincerely, Father James. Prison number 336, C Wing HMP Cragsville'

Hugh Wilberforce OBE, long serving governor of Gragsville high security prison, rubber stamped the letters for processing and smiled to himself. Good old Hatchet McGraw had been one of his greatest success stories. Now to see if Father James would find eight years in prison just as rewarding.

Hatchet McGraw went on to chair the Howard Penal reform committee where he was highly respected for his insightful attitude.

Six months after the letters, Father James was found dead in the prison chapel in mysterious circumstances. The police said they were not looking for anyone else in the case.

***

The castle in the air-
your mind is the key to the door.

His strong hands quickly flattened out the crumpled strip of note paper. It only took only a glance to realise that strength would be of no avail in solving this mystery. Nearby, a voice whispered who had written the note and it filled him with trepidation knowing how difficult it would be to maintain such high standards. He looked again at this quasi abstract gem of wisdom and knew the pressure was on to do it justice.

None of his experiences had prepared him for this task – a once in a lifetime opportunity to see if the spirits would lead his mind to a higher plane and guide his hand to pen such words that could convey to others what he thought he saw in them.

Later, when alone and all was quiet, he read again. . .

"At a glance they evoked a sense of the outdoors, of heritage and the past, and of adventure, of being here at home and yet also far away."

He considered each word in turn, then how they blended to hint of something different, something almost unworldly. The sentence was, in itself, harmonious yet filled with opposites. Not opposites in conflict, no, opposites in harmony. He then considered the author and why they might have written this text, hoping this would provide a clue to the answer. He knew there was always purpose behind the author's work but beyond this he knew little else.

What did seem apparent was that it represented a subtle, even coded, message, one of deep meaning. In fact, there were layers of meaning, some of which may prove unfathomable to his simple mind.

There was a spiritual tone to the message, something that spoke a silent wisdom to the soul, though the mind would never be able to explain why.

Pen in hand, he sat quietly, as the thinking mind was hushed to allow the divine oneness to whisper the answer in pictures.

This is what he saw.

A pea gravel drive stopped dead at some fine stone steps that in turn led to a studded oak door. Only what was shown could be seen, the building itself may have been a 16th century medium sized manor, but this is only a guess for what was beyond his viewable image always faded into nothingness.

The door was opened for him and a sense of invitation led him in. His boots were strangely silent on the hewed stone floor of a grand hallway. The hall was wide and high, ornate panels clad the walls and a central chandelier of oil lamps illuminated the grand staircase. Turning left into a large drawing room, we are amazed at the length of the resplendent velvet curtains, drawn back in the grand bay windows to illuminate the dark mahogany furniture. As our eyes survey the room and its opulent contents, we stop suddenly, aware that we are being watched. There, either side of an ornate marble fire surround, sat two huge animals. Carvings, so realistic that we expect them to move, carvings of what might be deer hounds. The mat black animals are as still as we are and as our eyes look on in surprise, their own amber eyes look back with a fearless knowing. Perhaps a wistful, far away knowing that they could never abandon.

We sense they represent the well-loved pets of some kindly owner from the past and that now they stand guard over their own heritage at spirit manor.

He paused from writing, sensing someone had entered the grand room from behind him. He turned sharply to see a dear little old lady in the doorway. She smiled and spoke, 'I suppose you have come to hear the rest of the story. Would you like a cup of tea first, Richard?'
He relaxed, smiled and replied, 'Why yes please, Ann, that would be lovely – do you have biscuits too?'

Written for an exercise at the Mulberry writing group.

***

The Spadger Gang.

They hang about my garden,
nicking all the food.
They've not once begged my pardon,
I think that's rather rude.

Around my costly food trough,
Some pretty birds do hang,
But they are hardly tough enough,
To beat the spadger gang

How can a tiny, spadger's belly,
Hold all that birdy seed,
'nough to fill a size twelve welly,
Now surely, that's just greed.

The feeder's full by nine each day
By half past ten it's not
this doesn't suit the spadger's way,
they leave, for neighbour's plot

I'll tell you what, then I must go,
Just one small nagging moan,
But please don't tell, I told you so,
'Why can't they buy their own ? '

***

The Journey of Hisato Khalid.

Born in London to a Japanese mother and Egyptian father.

Still honouring their own cultures, his loving parents brought Hisato up to embrace western society and adopt English as his first language. As a happy young child, he would often peacefully drift to sleep listening to his mother's storytelling, which without fail ended, *'and they all lived happy ever after.'*

The abiding memory that came with those childhood stories was to remain with Hisato for the rest of his life. He was a bright child, studied well and achieved excellent results at a prestigious university, where he studied philosophy and ancient history. To the joy of his aging parents, Hisato married a pretty young woman whose parents were wealthy entrepreneurs. She had an eye for material gains and made the most of her position in life to accumulate substantial wealth. Hisato was more spiritually inclined, believing that we can never truly own anything; we merely borrow it while we live. His views made no difference to what he perceived as his wife's obsessive behaviour with financial gain. A big house, social standing and an interesting and clever husband led to ever more success and no room for children. For Hisato this was not the dream life he'd desired from childhood. After his parents died, he knew it was time to move on.

He'd imagined his parents would live forever. After all, didn't the fairy stories promise this? He took little with him but a few necessities and a change of clothing. With a reasonable bank balance of his own and passport in hand, he set out for the lands of his ancestors. There he hoped to find the answers to immortality that abounded in eastern mythology. First stop, Cairo, then on to Luxor, where his Egyptian parentage, smattering of Arabic and extensive knowledge of ancient history made him a most welcome guest among the local people. He bonded well with boatman Mustafa Mohamed and spent several weeks staying at the family home. They were good days, good company, fine weather, simple healthy food and a chance to meet genuine minded seers of ancient mythology. But even the guides working the valley of Kings only had superficial knowledge and it soon became apparent that what Hisato was discovering, as interesting as it might be, was not taking him towards the edge of immortality. Mustapha and his family begged Hisato to stay. Why not? He could settle there, marry a fine and devoted wife and enjoy a long and happy life in Egypt. But such a life was not long enough to fulfil Hisato's dream. Many a tear was shed at the airport for his parting, as the aircraft took off for an interconnecting flight to Japan. Perhaps the spiritual city of Kyoto would bring him the answers he sought.

Once more, Hisato soon made friends by his humble ways, his knowledge of the ancients and the Japanese language which his mother had taught him. Hisato seemed frustrated at every turn; Kyoto had become superficially spiritual in order to attract tourist dollars. Hisato already knew as much as any of the priests, monks and scholars of their day and the only gain, was meeting with relatives of his mother. They felt blessed by his arrival; they could not have been more attentive and kinder to him. Old Uncle Morihiro, as Hisato knew him, made him welcome in his own home and soon secretly dreamed of marrying Hisato off to a beautiful Japanese woman and there, in the village, they would all live happily ever after, all family and friends together.

One night, as Hisato sat with Uncle Morihiro, he told him of his dreams to realise immortality, just as the ancient Gods had done. Uncle was deeply saddened by the conversation. Being a deep-thinking philosopher himself, he had found no reason to believe in the possibilities of immortality.

'Hisato, my dear boy,' he said with great affection, 'only the Gods are immortal and they, only so, while they live in the minds of our children and in their children. It is the destiny of man to die. Don't waste a good life by trying to avoid that which is inevitable, for indeed it is.'

But Hisato was **not** sure death was inevitable, there **must** be a way, if only he could find it. He was irritated that the very root of his beliefs, in the lands of his ancestors, failed to provide the answers he sought. He was by now short of money, having spent it on gurus, monks and mystics, but he had enough for one more flight. Hisato had already trawled the finest libraries and private collections for manuscripts that might help his quest. He had once read a quite plausible report of a Hermitage of Immortality near an obscure Tibetan/Mongolian border. Here would lay the answer, of this he was sure. Yes, this would be the place.

Once more, a happy family was to be saddened by his parting. With much begging and wringing of hands they watched him leave. Part of them died, for he'd taken a piece of their life away with him.

The journey to the Hermitage was long, much longer and harder than he ever imagined it could be. With his money soon gone, he fell on charity, begging lifts from drovers and other travelling folk. Much of it though, he walked. As the weeks wore on, his clothes were rags, his feet blistered through worn shoes and his joints ached with the sorrowful hunger for rest. In truth, this was a lonely, painful road and its only saving grace was his belief that, at the end, the secret of immortality awaited him.

Eventually, Hisato came within grasp of his destination and a villager pointed towards the distant greenery of a small valley amidst an otherwise barren and stony landscape. It took Hisato a whole day to arrive. By then the sun had dropped behind a mountain peak and he felt the cold bite into his bones. In front of him was a humble stone hovel showing thin wisps of smoke from a dwindling fire.

The hermit welcomed him in. It was hard to tell who looked the more ancient, as both had suffered much in search of their respective desires. Hisato was surprised to see how frail the Hermit appeared and obviously not a candidate for immortality. Weakened by the dust of his road and demoralised by this final disappointment, Hisato collapsed exhausted on the cold earthen floor. With the last remnant of his own life the Hermit eased Hisato's body onto the cot and sheltered him with sack cloth. Now all alone and in the dark, Hisato was just conscious when death came for him and tapped on the doorway of his soul. Hisato's search was over.

Post Script:
Hisato means - 'long lived', Khalid, - 'immortal';
His name and his upbringing, like a moth to a flame, enticed him towards an enchanting lamp that would never be lit for him.

***

The Therapists' Meeting.

It was her first meeting with the local therapist fraternity. Being closet transgender, she was suspicious of most people from the start and didn't expect to gain anything more than a biscuit and cup of tea at this strange event.

She sighed with a knowing disbelief when the leader of the group asked them to close their eyes and offer up a prayer of thanks to the universe. Instead, she stared around the room looking at the others, smirking at their odd mudra hand shapes and their pretentious smiles of celestial connection.

"Thank you," said the leader, who seemed to have more credentials than our new visitor had hot dinners however, our visiting guest remained very confident that only her therapy was the true one. After all, she'd paid for a course run by a retired Tibetan monk who lived on the nearby council estate. He'd proved to her that only he was connected to the Gods by demonstrating levitation in his kitchen. "Remember," he'd said, as she handed over the £500 fee in cash, "all the others are charlatans, you are now ready to heal the world with your knowledge, you are inducted, attuned and connected. Remember to set up the direct debit in order to maintain the connection." With that, he pressed a lucky rabbit's foot into her hands. *(Author's note; he had a drawer full of them, obtained as a job lot from the local poacher.)*

They all sat in a circle around a lit candle – one of those cheap smelly ones from the local gift shop. "Please introduce yourself to the group in turn," the leader asked. "Let's start with our new lady, Osiris."

"Damn," she thought, "better play this cool. "Well, Osiris is the spirit name bequeathed me through the

Tibetan book of the dead. I've just qualified as an expert healer but cannot tell you more as I was told by the founder to keep it a secret. If we tell, then we are disconnected from the one who knows all. You should really believe in my therapy," she said, furtively stroking the rabbit's foot three times in her pocket.

"Thank you," Osiris, "most interesting," the leader said, reminding herself of her morning's angel card which said 'Judgement.' "Next."

'Osiris' listened with a sense of aloofness and pity on these poor wretches, all no doubt duped out of their money by some charlatan. There was one young lady who was a dowser. Osiris thought, "Now correct me if I'm wrong, but I thought dowsing was done by old men in scruffy clothes looking to solve waterworks problems." Osiris struggled to hold back a snigger when the next, a middle-aged lady in smart country clothing said that she was into Shiatsu. 'Don't they realise Shiatsu is a Japanese poodle of some sort? My God, it's worse than I thought, I'm so glad I wasn't taken in by that one.'

Around the room they went, everyone pretending to be interested in alternative therapies, the only one who wasn't making some judgement was old Mrs McDougall, the herbalist, now in her eighties and stone deaf.

"Next."

"Hi, I'm Tracey and I'm into Reiki, following the late Dr JuJitsu from Amsterdam. Sadly, he died last year while experimenting with a vegan diet that predicated on mushrooms. I'm a Reiki 6 shihan and can offer you all a 50% discount." At which point she handed out some cards.

While the leader thanked Tracey and covertly screwed the card up into the hidden depths of her handbag, Osiris was confused, "Surely, if she's following her master she should be dead now and any way I'm sure I've seen a cereal called Raiky in the supermarket's 'free from' isle."

While contemplating the various weird names of modern cereals, she missed the name of the next speaker, not that it mattered as she was only another nutter. This time, an astrologist of all things. She remembered as a child looking at the astrology section of her father's Daily paper, it was always some general rubbish that applied to anyone with half a brain cell. "Oh, how do these poor people get caught up in such scams?" she asked herself.

The leader finished the meeting with a meditation, or muditation as Osiris' teacher had called it, for it usually made life even more irritating – unless you were 'connected' of course, like what she was.

As they said their goodbyes, Osiris silently vowed never to come back.

Strangely, it mirrored with welcome relief, the view of the leader, somewhat psychic herself.

No therapists were harmed in the making of this story. Yet.

***

The Tour Guide.

'A dream job,' they'd said at the interview, 'lots of tips, free accommodation and food thrown in, great bonus scheme and an adventure every time you step into the street.'

'I'll take it,' I said, 'when do I start?'

'Existing staff have first choice; we'll let you know in a couple of weeks what is left. One day, if you work hard you may become like the farmyard cockerel, king of the midden. Then **you** can choose first.'

It turned out that 'existing staff' included the boss's sister, two cousins and an illegal alien that worked for nothing and did him 'favours'. They chose the Russian Oligarch's Seychelles extravaganza which left me with an Italian peasant's weekend touring old London slums and the docks.

The boss hinted that if all went well, I might be given the 'Texans trash Monaco casino week'. If I did well!

I had a choice of arriving on the day, with mileage at three pence a mile or I could stay free in B&B at a back-street garret in Balham. I took the latter and was surprised to find it being run by the boss's mother. I'd stayed in better places in downtown Karachi. I spent the evening scouring the internet on dockland history, being constantly amazed by the rich plethora of amazing yet dubiously accurate information available – but it would do. Let's face it, I didn't speak a word of Italian and had severe doubts about their interest in English. This proved to be truer than I had imagined.

As I approached a huddle of early-morning damp and peckish visitors on the doorstep of our offices they recognised my name badge and surged forward. The badge proclaimed, **John Smith. Executive Guide. Utopian Tours**

for the Gifted. That's not my name. John Smith was a former employee, no longer with the company. The name badge and a couple of fingers had been returned by a Columbian tour group wanting to ransom him. They were obviously disappointed. They'd picked on the wrong company !

Apparently in order to be worthwhile having my own name badge made, I'd need at least three month's exemplary service.

It started well, my fears of losing one of my charges abated as I realised they were equally terrified of losing sight of me in this part of London. They clung to me like baby monkeys, even when I visited the public toilets at East Cheap tube station.

We weren't allowed in the docks proper. They had a security lock down in place. However, we were given access to some disused railway sidings that bordered a dry dock, (that wasn't anymore). It was good enough; we had a view of the river, the cranes, a few old ships and as the tide was out, lots of mud. We could also view the frenetic activities of the security forces in the working docks as they hunted down a tour group of a different sort – three stowaway rabid baboons had jumped ship from an Indian cargo vessel. I read in the Balham gazette later that the alpha male had already killed and eaten two crew members as they sailed through the Bay of Biscay.

A major highlight, which I told them in my best sign language, I had personally arranged, was a team from the bomb squad defusing a five-hundred-pound war time bomb out on the mud and surrounded by sandbags. A few of the group trained their cameras, no doubt hoping to make the BAFTAs or at least a few coins off the news channels when it exploded. As they hadn't eaten for about twenty-four hours by now, I took them to a quaint Italian restaurant, *'The Cosy Nostra'*, with whom the company had an account. In the beginning my group were excited but it faded when they found out it was run by an Albanian with Polish waiters. The factory-delivered pizzas from Brazil looked okay to me but the group picked all the pineapple bits off as well as some other things they didn't recognise. I didn't eat as I was still a bit queasy from my breakfast.

As per their Mediterranean habit they spent the afternoon dozing in the maritime museum tea rooms.

Next day, most of the group were being detained for questioning at Romney Marsh police station while a search was made for the three that had gone missing. We eventually found them. One had joined *'The Cosy Nostra'* as a genuine Sicilian bouncer and the other two were in the process of setting up their own Tour Company. I mean, how hard can it be?

The boss was less than pleased, despite no one dying and all being found in the end. I didn't get a bonus and wages were deducted to pay for some undeclared expenses.

Sorry I can't stop as I want to catch the doctors before they close, about the bites and rash I think may well have come from the B&B.

***

Suspicion.

A rural Edwardian tale of adversity and
courage during hard times.

The oil lamp hanging from the beam swung wildly on its hook and the flame flickered desperately as the old Inn door opened to the wild night, hurriedly ushering in a wind battered visitor.

Old Seth the village mole-catcher pushed his body hard against the door to close it tight and secure the latch. 'By God,' he said, 'that be devilish windy this night it be.'

'No moles to be caught tonight then Seth,' joked the burly innkeeper, pouring him a tankard of ale from the big jug.

'If I know ee moles, they'll take advantage of this bad weather and be all over his Lordship's lawn by tea time come morning's night,' muttered Seth and, like a pack of hunting wolves, the wind around the ill-fitting windows howled in accord.

Seth shuffled his old boots across the sawdust floor and sat in his favourite chair. Nearby, were four men, strangers they were, and though next to the inglenook wood fire they still wore their great coats with collars turned up. Caps, the mark of a working man, covered their heads, and their boots looked the worse for wear. Occasionally a gust of wind forced smoke down the chimney, oblivious, the men talked on, absorbed deeply in their secretive liaison.

Seth's friendly greeting, 'Eeenin to ee gents,' was largely ignored, only one man, the larger of the four thickset men, grunted back, 'An' yerself squire,' then quickly turned his face away for the work in hand.

'Ah well,' mused Seth, 'obviously strangers, not a local accent, seemed sort of … well, not sure really … anyway, strangers they were and mean looking ones at that … wouldn't want to meet them on a dark night.'

Seth supped his ale in a peace of his own making. Now Old Seth might have been getting long in the tooth but there was nothing wrong with his hearing. Some said he could hear moles moving underground – some even said he talked to them. Though some would also say, 'old wive's tales mostly – mostly'.

Seth didn't hear all that was being said, he just caught bits of the conversation; 'gotta get money soon', 'counting on us, back 'ome', 'take our chances when we can I say', 'what about the rich geezer's big house down the road', ' shh, not so loud.' …..

William, the big innkeeper, came close and placed a callused and powerful hand on old Seth's shoulder, the hand of part time village blacksmith, 'See 'ere old Seth, I'm putting ee another fine log on the fire to keep ee warm and happy. Now don't ee forget that kindness when ee next sees his Lordship's woodsmen.'

'Ar, to be certain, there's always plenty of useful men about at his Lordship's,' Seth said, loud enough so as the four men could not fail to hear. At the same time, he spoke to William with his eyes, indicating his distrust of the strangers with a sideways look and an enquiring expression.

Seth went back to the bar with William on the excuse of obtaining more ale, but as they huddled over the bar it was other things that occupied their minds. For some half hour they chewed over what they should do about their suspicions but before they could decide, the Inn door burst open. Standing in the open doorway, with no intention of closing it, was one of his Lordship the Earl's gardeners, 'Big trouble up at the House and we need help quick.'

By now he has the attention of everyone in the Inn, including the four strangers who are now all looking straight at the gardener with earnest intent.

'What's wrong, old chap?' asked William, peering past the wind flickered lantern.

'Fire, Fire, ... stables on fire ... the horses trapped ... his Lordship is begging for help to save his horses ..... will you come?'

'We're on our way old chap, we're on our way.' As William threw on his rough old coat, he shouted at the strangers, 'I'm sorry lads, but us have got to go, ye'll have to leave the Inn, I'm sorry.'

The men stood quickly in unison.
'Nah worries guv, we're coming wiv yer,' shouted back the big fellow. With heavy chairs pushed back like they were feathers, they all reached the door together and out into the dark night. William grabbed two lanterns and they set off hurriedly on the gravelled mile to the manor house.

Soon they were close enough to smell the fire and hear the horses' tortured cries of fear.

It was a scene of total chaos at the stables; stone built of two stories, the stalls being on the ground floor and storage above, wooden beams, floors and walls everywhere. Straw and winter hay were well alight with ever thickening dark yellow smoke, servants ran and shouted, even the kitchen girls were there ... not that any could do much to help.

William, Seth and the strangers found his Lordship by the closed main door to the stables. Though quite beside himself with pain for an impending and horrific death of his beloved horses, he managed to explain, 'Fire, started in loft, burnt through floor, far end of stables, the end where we usually get in, horses down this end but we can't open doors from here ... only from inside. The way through is barred by fallen beams and fire .. My God, just listen to those poor creatures. What can we do?'

'If it can be done sir, it will be done, ee have my word on it,' William said, with more than a note of fervent promise in his voice. And with that, the six moved as one to the burning end of the building. There was a small bucket chain from the well in use, but to little avail, they would never extinguish such flames, the only hope was to open the doors from the inside and save the horses, for the barn was already condemned to a fiery hell. William and the big fellow looked through the door together, much of the fire was still on the upper floors, tiles could be heard breaking on the floor above as parts of the roof failed, in front of them, a few feet in, was some smoking, water damped straw and a muddle of fallen timbers, some of them huge beams of oak.

William turned to the big fellow and said, 'Look, I can't do this on my own, but I reckon it's clear past this point and I feel I can open they far doors an let they horses out. Can you, ... will you ... help me by yon beams?'

'Count on us squire, what we've been through in life, we ain't afraid.' Pulling their collars higher and wrapping some old hemp sacking around their hands and arms they entered through the doorway to hell.

'Seth,' shouted William, 'get ee to the main door, tell his Lordship to be ready for they horses.' And with that, he disappeared choking into the yellow grey smoke.

Seth glanced in horror as five men disappeared from sight as if gone forever. He hoped upon hope that the building would stand long enough for William to do his work, he then, quick as old bones would let him, went to find his Lordship.

Strong as William was, the beam that barred his way was beyond his strength, as he crouched low to gain some fresher breath for one last attempt, he heard the big fellow shout, 'go for it mate, we can't hold it up much longer.' William saw through stinging, tear blinded, eyes the four strangers had lifted the beam enough for him to get through. He didn't waste a second, for with every second he was getting weaker and more confused. As he'd hoped, it was cleaner air further down the stables, he followed the stall fronts on the left to the great doorway and, fumbling with shaking but powerful hands, he found the bolts and locking bar that freed the door to open. With an almighty shove, fresh air rushed in to greet him as the heavy door swung open.

As good as his word Seth was prepared, along with the stable boys and his Lordship, to guide the frenzied horses away to safety. It was going well, despite the horses being panicked and some kicking out, they were all released safe to a corner field.

'Let it burn now, let it burn,' called his Lordship, 'don't risk yourselves anymore, my beautiful horses are safe, God bless you all for your help.'

His composure soon regained, his Lordship ordered the kitchen staff to prepare refreshments for his helpers, and for everyone to stand back from the now collapsing building. The roof caved in first and carried the first floor down with it, the falling twisting beams levered the stone walls as they fell, and it was all but over for the old stables.

It was a smoke laden and sweat smelly throng that gathered in the great kitchen, his Lordship mingled with his servants like they were bosom friends, the like of which was never seen before, nor since.

'William, Seth, good friends that you are, heroes both that you are, you will know my gratitude in the days to come, you can be sure of that,' beamed his Lordship, who had been liberal with the port as much as with his thanks.

Seth drew his Lordship aside, 'what of they four strangers, milord, I'm not seeing they since the fire, perhaps they need a watching sir.'

'Nay Seth, good men all, they saved the day for us with their strength and camaraderie, without their bravery our noble William could not have prevailed against the odds as he did. Good men all, simple working folk, iron ore miners walking their way to Northamptonshire for the promise of work to feed their families. I've had the butler sort them out some fresh clothes ... not burnt ones, eh? ... Here they come now. Here lads, here, come join us for a meal,' he called.

They sat about the great pine table, food and drink a plenty, there they sat, his Lordship the Earl, the mole-catcher, the black-smith and ... no, not four strangers any more, just four good men that could look any other in the eye and tell their tale of heroism.

But I doubt they ever would, so here,
I have done it for them.

***

The Tramp and the Priest. – a moral paradox.

The new incumbent watched with apparent concern as the collection plate was ponderously circulated among the congregation, "please give generously, and remember the poor, the homeless, and the needy. Remember those that don't enjoy the good life you may have and put a little extra gift in this week, thank you," implored his finely trained religious tone. His years in the clergy had given him the skill to observe body language of the givers and the sneaky non givers. He wouldn't mind promising eternal damnation to the rich who kept their money in their pockets but noisily fumbled the change on the plate to give an appearance of generosity.

It was a new church building and the clergy's substantial modern residence was attached. In fact, he didn't even have to walk in the rain to reach his place of work; I mean worship, as there was an interconnecting door. Of course, he had the services of a housekeeper and the gardens were tended by contractors or for free by keen parishioners hoping for a front seat in the gardens of heaven. There was a large car park by the side of the church which then backed on to substantial gardens and the usual garden shed . . . a fine shed it was too by all accounts.

It wasn't unknown for this honourable man of the cloth to be invited to parishioner's homes for the odd dinner and a glass or two of the hard stuff. It was during one of these salubrious sojourns that he confessed to finding a tramp in his shed, the church's shed. The church, a place of sanctuary and spiritual succour, its shed reduced to a 'no room at the Inn' establishment. The tramp was a well-known figure in the town, his appearance was so unusual that once seen, not forgotten. A portly bald man of great stature wearing long flowing clothes tied around the waist with a soft rope that would easily be at home in a Buddhist monastery, over his shoulder he was always carrying a large round bundle wrapped up in what seemed to be a blanket, presumably the sum total of his life's belongings. He was a clean looking, contented man who always appeared to be happy with his lot in life. Sadly our man of the cloth was not so happy with a monk like nomad occupying his shed ! He explained this to us over a few whiskies, a beef casserole and double helping of Tiramisu. The new incumbent had asked the tramp to leave his little wooden sanctuary, despite knowing full well that the previous religious resident of the manse had always welcomed the old tramp whenever he had returned to the city and was indeed happy to offer him shelter in the church's garden shed.

Well the cat was truly out of the bag now; it was somewhat of a mistake to make such a confession . . . particularly in this household!

When Christmas came around and cards were bought, a most suitable one offered itself without hesitation for our friend of the cloth. It was a beauty, one of those old Flemish paintings of frozen rivers and the like. This particular one had some grand gate posts and gates to a fine driveway on the left, centre was a tent pitched on a frozen river with a few men standing outside in apparent conversation. It was perfect, couldn't have been more so. Inside the card he wrote "Happy Christmas, hope you like the card. It shows the gates to a Bishop's Palace and some of his burly and well-fed henchmen evicting a starving tramp from his tattered tent because he was making the view from the gate untidy."

The moral paradox persists, contemplated no doubt more in depth by the tramp who walks his path than the priest who walks nowhere but keeps a steady watch over his empty, lifeless shed.

***

Turkey and Tinsel.
A day out.

The newly formed Goodtimes coaching company wasn't averse to running a turkey and tinsel trip at any time of the year, probably because they were new to the business. Now, the Fluffy Bunny writing club of north Devon knew a good thing when they saw it and booked a coach for the 23rd of May.

There weren't enough of them to fill a coach, so they opened it up to the public.

Who knows, they might even sell a few copies of their anthology, 'Tales from the fluffy side.'

One such member of the public who purchased a ticket was Crystal Lovemore, travelling under an assumed name. With a long red dress over an ample, muscular body, wearing sunglasses that rested under the fringe of one of those bright green page boy style wigs, Crystal took a seat half way down the coach and next to a window from which an overly excited reflection smiled back in admiration.

John the driver, in fact the only driver the company had, switched on the mike and spoke, 'Here we go then ladies and gents, hold on to your wallets and hats and let's go and have a *bleeping* good time. My wife has made some sandwiches and will bring them around at the halfway mark. *Bleeping* lovely they are and dead cheap at a fiver each.' John belched and switched off the mike.

Except for Jennifer, who was busy stifling the sniggers brought about by John's swearing and memories of boarding school in upper Zululand, leading members of the Fluffy Bunny Writers shuddered at such language and certainly would not be purchasing sandwiches. In any case they had brought the club's old biscuit tin with them.

 Behind Barbara and Di, Crystal sat fidgeting excitedly on the mock leather seat. A cultured warm voice from behind Crystal increased the tension. 'Good morning dear young lady, I see you are travelling alone, as am I, perhaps I can join you.' Crystal blushed at the thought but before able to answer the fine gentleman with the suave voice, he had already lifted his surfer's rucksack off the parcel shelf and made his unsteady way into the aisle. Unsteadiness could be due to a surfeit of Dead Bunny country cider or John's driving – as it was the first time out for him in a full size coach. (I mean, how difficult can it be?)

Crystal grimaced at the sight of this huge bearded tramp like creature that blotted out the sun as he leant over to replace his rucksack on the rack. As he leant ever closer, his short and dinner stained T shirt rode up and a hairy belly smelling of spilled curry pressed its fatty weight into

Crystal's face. Eventually he sat down, his bulk pressing Crystal towards the window. Then, with a firm hand on Crystal's thigh, he introduced himself, 'My name's Bob, but most people use my nickname, Groper. I'm a surfer you know and couldn't believe my luck to get a cheap ticket like this to Croyde.' Patting Crystal's legs again, 'My you've got some fine thigh muscles under that pretty dress, surfing? Horse riding? Wrestling?' Groper laughed at the thought and as he did so, a globule of last night's curry shot out of his mouth and stuck to Crystal's sunglasses. Crystal was forced by secret circumstances, to endure the presence of this overweight surfing oaf in silence. A silence that Groper decided was an open invitation.

The coach mike crackled into action again, a loose wire having a life of its own, 'We're stopping for a few minutes in Braunton, as we're running out of *bleeping* fuel and the missus needs a wee. Feel free to wander about the garage a while but don't be late back to the *bleeping* bus.' Another good belch and the speaker crackled off, sounding like it might have worked its magic for the last time.

'Excuse me,' asked Crystal, making an obvious attempt to break free and leave. Groper was even more reluctant to move now as he was immediately enamoured of Crystal's husky and to him surprisingly seductive voice. However, in the end and a bit taken back by Crystal's determination and strength, Groper stepped backwards into the aisle, loudly passing wind through his ancient tracksuit as he did so.

A much relieved but by now mentally scarred Crystal, booked a taxi at the garage and returned home immediately.

As the Fluffy Bunny group returned to their seats, Elizabeth moved quickly to rescue Sally from an erstwhile new travelling companion, leaving Groper the bearded surfer to scan empty seats for another lone woman. Susie was purely by chance the lucky recipient, as Barbara had taken too long to return from the shop and buying herself a bag of Bon Bons.

Finding her seat at the front of the coach taken, Barbara collected her notebook and knitting, 'It's okay Susie, I'll go and sit with Ann, you enjoy the rest of the trip with this nice young man,' she said, rustling the sweetie bag and peering lengthily and half sightedly over her specs at the happy couple.

In a quiet terraced house some ten miles away, odd socked feet rested on a coffee table. Reclining on the sofa, dressed only in socks and underpants with legs akimbo, a can of lager in one hand and a bag of crisps in the other, Bob Lovemore swore he that would never, never, ever again wear his wife's clothes in public.

'Stuff the *bleeping* turkey and tinsel,' he thought, 'and the *bleeping* surfers, and the *bleeping* fluffy bunnies too. Stuff 'em all.'

He changed the channel to watch a good old war film and slurped at his lager, by the time his wife came back from a business trip he would have forgotten all about it. Not so the Fluffy Bunny writing group, many of whom are still in therapy to this day.

***

Firewood on the far side.

There they were, on the other side.
Across the river, they did hide,
tempting logs for winter's use,
but bridge was gone, and cooked his goose.

Along the narrow track he trudged,
Some, mighty logs, could not be budged,
Though few, with effort, he could lift
And used his car to homeward, shift.

***

To Serve

There will always be that someone prepared to step into the dark and the unknown; their sense of duty far greater than the common desire to stay in comfort. They will enter the winter cold in place of others that prefer the warmth, company and music. Without their sacrifice, there would be no party. They are humble, self-effacing and serve with nobility of purpose, quiet and unnoticed by the many.
They are the, someone to stand in the rain, and fetch you from that train, someone to reach into the fire, to serve and never tire.

Too old for a funeral.

As if his very life depended upon it, he rushed to the computer to view the next awe inspiring and vitally important message that the bleeps told him had just arrived.

It was Judi, - a disappointment. 'What does she want now?' he thought. None the less he read on, you never know your luck, do you?

Judi was writing to say her car was indisposed, it had shown an 'engine failure' warning on the dash and was now at that awful garage that charges so much for repairs – but it's near the hairdressers. She couldn't understand why it had failed as she vacuumed the car every week and paid the Romanian chap once a fortnight to wash and polish it.

He knew why it failed – Judi's mechanical skills ran to fuelling it occasionally and even then, needing help to unlock the fuel filler cap. It might have helped if she learned how to use all the gears and operate the clutch fully. Never mind.

Judi needed the use of a car to take a 92-year-old to a funeral.

'It'll probably be his, knowing her driving.' he thought. Adding to himself, 'it won't be my car she's using. I'll ignore that bit.'

He stared blankly at the screen, his mind on funerals. Funerals eh? He'd seen 'em all. A day dream gently carried him far away to a place and time he'd been before . . . it was Cambridge crematorium, an afternoon funeral . . . he was one of three bearers assisting the funeral director (who happened to be a local builder, as many were in the old days.)

At the foot of the coffin on the right stood himself and, on the left,, Ray Goodfellow, a short, elderly, some would say refined gentleman and retired carrot factory manager. At the head of the coffin stood Daniel Brutus, a very large man whose own frugal living was made as a minister of some obscure church. As the foot of the coffin was lifted on to the rollers, he could see that Ray was in some sort of distress, as he'd stopped moving and was looking downwards. "Are you all right, Ray?" He asked with genuine concern for this kindly old gentleman. Who knows, it could be his heart. Ray was not to answer before big Brutus had lifted the head of the coffin and, oblivious to anything else, launched it with awesome force onto the rollers. Even as Ray staggered back, doubled up and twisting away, big Brutus didn't notice anything, he was away somewhere in his own cerebral vacant plot. As Ray recovered somewhat and turned back, the mourners had begun to file in through the open door, the problem was evident immediately. The sharp corner of the coffin had caught in the groin area of the poor man's trousers and Brutus' thought free, yet powerful launch, had mercilessly ripped off a goodly chunk of our friend Ray's best suit.

 Mourners and bereaved were now close by. It was too late to laugh.

To this day the reverend Daniel Brutus is still no doubt blissfully unaware of his part in Ray's downfall, well his trousers anyway, part of which would be cremated along with the deceased.

The computer bleeped loudly, frenziedly. Immediately he returned to the land of the living, dealing with yet another urgently un-ignorable and life changing missive from the electronic ether. Where would we be without it?

Two acts of random kindness.

After a working lifetime risking his life in the service of others, he was at last retired and free to live out more peaceful days sitting by his little beach hut, watching the world go by and enjoying the sea air. It became a pleasing habit to engage with walkers passing along the adjacent cliff top path.

One day a middle-aged couple stopped nearby to take photos. 'Would you like one with both of you in it?' he asked with a smile.

The woman smiled in return, mouthing 'Yes please.'

The man, however, did not seem so pleased and made no reply.

'Are you local,' our friend enquired, 'or just visitors?'

The woman replied with another smile and said they lived in the village, the cottage near the old inn. She was interrupted by an elbow in her ribs. 'We like to keep ourselves to ourselves. I'll thank you for our camera back and we'll be on our way,' her partner snarled.

Later, as he walked into the village to find lunch, he saw the couple again, this time on the beach and seemingly in a heated argument, the man agitatedly raising his arms and pointing aggressively towards the beach huts. Our friend stopped for a while, wondering if a second random act of kindness would be required of him that day. After a few minutes all seemed to calm down. He half suspected that he'd been seen.

On his way back to the sanctuary of his little hut, he was to meet the couple a third time. The man had a firm grip on the woman's elbow and made a great show of glaring intently in our friend's direction.

The rest of the afternoon passed with a few disturbed thoughts but no incident. He drove home to watch his favourite team play in a big match on TV. A couple of glasses of red wine and his feet up in a comfy chair awaited him.

It must have been about eleven in the evening, he thought he'd heard the doorbell earlier but now there was definitely a heavy impatient knocking at his front door. He even thought he'd glimpsed a furtive figure through his kitchen window, as he stood and made his way cautiously towards the sound of a closed fist beating on wood. As he came closer he heard, as no doubt embarrassingly would all of his neighbours within earshot, **'Police, open up!'**

He slowly opened the door, only to be pushed back inside his home by a burly, tattooed police officer, obviously high on adrenalin and screaming, **'Police, Police,'** at the top of his voice. The officer pressed even closer, staring wild eyed at our now very confused friend, '**Police**,' repeated the uniformed intruder, obviously enjoying every minute of it, 'We're investigating a stalker in a nearby village, and you fit the description, tall, bald and dopey looking. Now calm yourself down while I read you your rights.' Our now fearful friend was sure he overheard, 'you filthy scum,' muttered more quietly at the close of sentence.

He backed away from the officer.

'I think we'd better cuff you . . . for your own safety.' By now three more hob-nailed neo-fascist officers had forced their way into his home. 'Better do as you're told,' said one, tweaking the handle on his pepper spray.

The poor old chap soon found himself gasping for breath, his eyes stung like they were being thrashed with nettles and the heavy knee of an over-zealous arresting officer crushed his head into the carpet while screaming, 'relax, relax, stop resisting.'

After a miserable night in the cells he was released on bail until the next available magistrates' sessions.

On the day of the trial the case of stalking was dismissed immediately as the complainant had withdrawn all charges on psychiatric advice.

However, on other charges, he was found guilty of resisting arrest, failing to obey a lawful order, assaulting an officer of the law and acting in a manner such as to pervert the cause of justice.

'Guilty,' triumphantly proclaimed the smiling judge, a closet transvestite who kept his own tattoos and deviant attitudes well hidden and had only taken the job because he thought a wig came with it, 'Sentenced to four years. But as a random act of kindness I shall recommend an open prison and I hope you will appreciate this benevolent gift and learn from my example. Take him down, officer.'

Struck, using the magistrate's almost orgasmic judicial power, the sound of the gavel echoed in our friend's ears, reverberated by the sound of jail doors slamming in long empty corridors through the rest of his life.

How suspicious we are of kindness . . . such a shame.

***

The second chance.

Based on real events, real people, my people.

It was Saturday morning before six am, the 28th May 1887 and along with his sons and nearly 200 other miners, James Richmond was preparing to go underground.

James was a widower living at High Blantyre and at age fifty-eight was past his prime for coal pit working but the pay (at today's equivalent of 16 pence an hour) was better than nothing, which was the second of two unenviable choices.

Many a time James reflected on his Irish past and that of his ancestors. He thought on his grandparents, who in better times owned farms in County Antrim and once sailed lime ships across the Irish Sea. The great potato famine of 1845, which he'd barely survived as a young man of fifteen, had diminished any family wealth and those same grandparents were destined for a pauper's grave on Scottish soil. They were too old and weak to take their second chance of building a new life in Scotland. Nearly all the family became coal or iron ore miners; it was the only way to earn a living, if you could call it that.

James and one of his sons, John age 25, stood together by the cage of one of three lift shafts. Little did they know that within 3 hours it would stop working. In the semi gloom, weary eyes drained of life's joys looked around at once fit men, now with crippled fingers and dust choked lungs.

But they were comrades all, bonded in the face of a common adversary.

Omen like, James' safety lamp flickered and went out. He hurriedly returned to the pit head storekeeper and showed him the dead lamp.

"Give it here, I'll try it again and if it doesn't work, you'll have to miss this shift." The lamp gasped at its second chance and spluttered into life.

Not long after, the unlucky lamp was illuminating a coal seam some 130 fathoms below ground. (780 feet)

With picks, shovels and bare hands they toiled tirelessly to earn a pittance from the rich and distant mine owners to whom they were all but slaves.

At 9 o'clock it was break time underground, they downed tools and ate their breakfast in the gloom and all-pervading smell of coal stale air. At approximately 7 minutes past 9, the ground shook and dust filled the air - a dust that would carry the fire through much of the mine workings. The lucky ones died instantly from an explosion that destroyed everything in its path. 182 men were in the pit at that time. 73 would die, 53 from burns and 20 asphyxiated. The latter were brought to the surface with calm on their faces, entreating the unknowing observer to think their deaths had been peaceful. Trust me, this would have been far from the truth, but it was better the wives and mothers think otherwise.

The fire that issued from the mine, ignited the pit head gearing and jammed all the cages. It was four hours before an exploratory party could access the mine, to save the living and recover the dead. Miners from other pits in the Hamilton district rushed to assist, for the Udston mine workers had been shocked and decimated.

Regrettably, none of this need have happened. The explosion was later deemed caused by unauthorised blasting without properly checking for the miner's insidious old enemy, firedamp. (Methane gas)

But what of James? Did he survive? His lifeless body was brought to the surface along with his son John. Though terribly shaken and bleeding from the mouth, John survived. He had tried to save his father but had been overcome by fumes, though he had succeeded in saving a younger brother.

John and his brother lived on to take their second chance at life, working once more in the pit that had claimed the lives of their father and friends.

Four of the men who were pulled from the pit alive and sent home were to die later the same day – their own second chance revoked. Such events we call disasters, but that word is a trifling euphemism for the reality.

Forty-five hours after the explosion, almost all of the bodies had been recovered and at the bottom of pit 2, after nearly two days among their gruesomely deceased comrades, unbelievably two men still lived to tell their tale. The tale of a second chance.

***

Was it the mushrooms?

Visions and voices came and went, along with his fleeting consciousness. One minute, clarity, the next a fog of pain. Everything was confusion, reality blurred. He saw himself walking joyfully into one of those factory food pubs, the sort that lures in the gullible all-day drinkers and breakfast seekers. Yes, that was it; it was beginning to come back to him. Slowly, scraps of delusion joined together interspersed with bouts of pain induced unconsciousness.

During the next hour he felt floating sensations, saw blurred lights passing by overhead and heard the trundle of wheels, evocative of a childhood train journey. (He wasn't a good traveller then, either!)
He pulled a chair from under the table. In the dim mood lighting, designed to save electricity and hide the food, he admired the choice of seat covering. A swirled pattern that made any urine stains look like they were supposed to be there. His train went into a tunnel and when it came out there was an angel dressed in black with his breakfast. "Is there anything else, sir? she smiled.
As he forked a lump of hash brown about in the runny white of an anaemic egg, he thoughtfully observed two artificial sausages that seemed to be returning the stare. The cooking marks were identical. On closer scrutiny, it was apparent that the 'cooking marks' were pre-dyed into the recycled plastic skin. No need to pay a chef when a microwave would do the job. As he chewed doggedly on half a sausage, his fork found a new object of forensic interest, a remnant of tomato that had once seen better days, like sometime last year.
He'd had enough. He called for the manager and gave him a piece of his mind along with a sliver of gristle that shot

out of his mouth into the darkness of the mood lighting. Perhaps he'd gone too far, he felt himself being lifted. Oh no, was he being carried out by the bouncers? And he'd not finished his breakfast yet.

He felt himself flying through the air but the landing was soft. A bloke who seemed to be wearing some sort of blue dress shouted at someone nearby, "Six mls of adrenalin and stomach pump from ICU – be quick or we'll lose him."

From his drowsy bed at St Clare's, as dawn broke over the town, he could see through the hospital window the afore visited pub in all its superficial grandeur.

He wouldn't be having breakfast today – nor lunch either and certainly not there. . . ever again.

***

What's in a name?

I'll tell you, everything and nothing. Nothing, because a named object quite naturally can exist inherently without a name – a name incidentally that is not shared by most of the world. Inuits have thirty names for snow, Egyptians, none. So, what meaning has the name? None.

Language is imperfect for this reason and more deeply, it lacks the ability to describe spiritual enlightenment, the words simply do not exist. 'He who knows does not speak, he who speaks does not know'; a saying, based on this truth. Then what of the name of truth? Each of us has their own truth, and yet all of them are different.

How many Christians are called Herod, how popular is Oliver to Irish Catholics, how often will you hear, 'Come here Adolf,' to a little boy in Jerusalem? Genghis, Attila, Lucrecia, Barbara, how many choose these for their children. Chloe, Becky, Angela, all conjure up the image of pretty, talented young things but they might just as well be wizened old battle axes. So, the name can confuse, manipulate and cheat you by the stereotype held so dearly.

Once, in Russia on a martial arts trip, a pal of mine, Big Pete or Balshoi Piotre in Russian, was practicing his tiny grasp of Russian. The word for light sky blue is 'galabeya'. To show his knowledge he stood in front of a Russian chap (homophobic to a man) tapped him on his blue T shirted chest and asked, 'Galibeya?' This caused some consternation and subsequent amusement when he found out that the word was used to describe gay people. (As is Pitoch, or Cockerel).

Names can tell intimate secrets, eg children growing up with strange names that speak of past indiscretions. Or their drunken father ignored his wife's choice of name and the young lad grows up called Millwall or Ranger or worse still some foreign unspellable player's name so everyone thinks he was illegitimate.

Then there are the parents who don't think too carefully … or do they… about name reversal. Registers are often surname first. So, someone called William Big will soon be known as Big Willy – for the rest of his tortured life. Donna Bella, Abigail Downton, Conan Barking. (Conan is Irish for little hound.)

There's so much more fun to have but I have to leave for my therapist's now.

***

Writer's Block? Some advice.

First, never worry; it will only make matters worse. I mean, is it so important your writing is worthy of publication? No; Best to write for yourself, because quite frankly hardly anyone apart from your own mother is remotely interested and even that might be in doubt.

However, let's not be negative about your inadequacies. Let's see if we can at least manage a vestige of literary refinement in your otherwise drab current attempts.

You need a good subject, something deeply meaningful to write about with soul, with passion. Or, something everyday perhaps, routine and mundane but to which others can relate. Always have a good beginning and a good ending, the middle bit should be at least passable in order that the reader lasts long enough to find the good ending. Always describe the scenes with colourful adjectives; guide the reader step by step with the finest detail leaving no doubt in their mind as to what was in your own when you wrote it. Having said that, always leave some space for the reader's imagination. Keep your language simple, avoiding equivocal and nebulous complexities to the recalcitrant authors. But avoid writing so simply that you appear to look down on your reader as though a mental age of six flatters them. Try poetry . . . or not as the mood or ability takes you. Some prefer rhyming some not, so whatever you write you are bound to annoy at least fifty per cent of any readers that deign to lower themselves and select your work as worthy. Simple covers work best but regardless of whether it is a treatise on Einstein's wife's counter theories on dark matter or a cookery book for dyslexic cross dressing bachelors, then the best cover of all is an evocative, alluring picture of a pretty woman . . . the only cover which is guaranteed to attract interest . . . until they read your text of course. Be truthful at all times unless you suspect prosecution to follow. In any event be generous to yourself in the biography section. Trust me; they will not know you did not work for MI6. No one knows that I did, before moving to help NASA with the Mars landing security section. Along with my diving career recovering Spanish gold in the West Indies these are the sort of things you need never tell. After all you don't want to attract burglars, only readers. Don't write too long a story but neither make it too short. People like humour and happy endings yet pathos and intrigue also appeal, along with soul searching and inspiration. Remember that your reader may be totally thick or possibly in contrast a lot brighter than you. So, don't spell out the plot and ruin the surprise yet don't make it so obscure that they still can't understand it when the surprise is sprung. Try not to listen to others too much. What do they know? But instead listen carefully to good advice imbued in such learned articles as this one.

Finally, good luck. Because you sure as hell are going to need a heap of it, as well as relatives in the publishing business . . . ones that actually like you !

***

You are the sunshine ... continued
(Continued from some other author about a guy's precious yellow mini car so I'm afraid you can't read it.)

With a thousand vintage ccs purring away like a sunbathing tiger on the warm tarmac drive, he closed the squealing garage door behind him. Several passers-by and a neighbour turned to stare and he made a mental note to oil the mechanism on his return – that's if he did return that night ! With his wife away, having taken the children for their summer holidays to his mother-in-law who ran Brunhilda's new age colonic irrigation boot camp in Buleemia, his middle age crisis was in full swing and he had signed up to one of those selective dating agencies. Definitely not the sort of agency that when the lady asks for a tall, quiet, dark, well-built vegetarian, they fix her up with a Gorilla. No, this was a great agency, very discreet, selective and best of all, cheap too. He'd gone for, youngish, timid, compliant blond, preferably good cook, liked ironing and was short sighted. He was in luck, the agency had only one like this on the books and she was back on the market again after spending three years away, somewhere about which they didn't care to elaborate.

'Probably worked abroad,' he mused.

He'd lied just a little on his own dating profile. He may have knocked a few years off and exaggerated his education and profession a little. He just hoped she didn't ask him to play the guitar, which he'd now regrettably said he'd learned from Eric Clapton. Truth to be told, he was tone deaf and had butter fingers.

They met at a cosy little restaurant, secluded from the main thoroughfare, (read, dimly lit, back street dump). Lucky for him, vanity had convinced her to leave her glasses at home. Lucky for her, his own eyesight was on the way out too and while she remained sitting it gave no clue as to how short and plump she was. The evening went well; he had parked on the pavement just outside the restaurant window to keep an eye on the real love of his life. God, this was his lucky night, she seemed to be on a diet of some sort and this would be a cheap bill. She too was preoccupied by the little yellow mini and hardly took her eyes off it except for the odd occasion when she squinted, half blind across the table to watch as he wiped slopped soup off his tie. 'My goodness,' she thought, 'could this be **the** Rowan Atkinson? '

They were just about to leave and at the point where his thoughts turned to if she might pay half and what she was like in bed, when horror of horrors, the evil dead came walking down the street. Yes … a traffic warden! He must move fast, but he daren't leave without paying . . . it wasn't the sort of place you skipped out of, not if you valued your kneecaps or liver. 'Please, don't let them take my sunshine away, here's the keys, just move it down the street a bit while I pay,' with that he threw the keys. She caught them with the deftness of a trained circus baboon and was gone in a flash of yellow sequinned mini skirt and orange trainers.

He quickly paid, leaving a half reasonable tip in case he brought his new date back one day for afters.

Once outside, he stood suddenly alone, twitching nervously in the evening darkness and peering down the road. He could see no lights, no precious yellow mini, no one but a shuffling vagrant wearing a warden's uniform jacket he'd found in a bin behind the police station.

Without taxi fare, he took the long bus ride home, for he never took much money out with him on a date. His front door was already open, his home devoid of all valuables. A light was on in the kitchen, he rushed through thinking she might be playing a joke. There was only a badly spelled note, 'Thanks for a lovely evening, we must do it again sometime, Kat Burglar, The Scrubs, London. xxx'

What would his wife say when she saw everything was gone, even her silver trophy for mixed mud wrestling and gilt framed GCSE butchery certificate were missing.

But worst of all for him, would he ever see his sunshine again?

***

First day – new job

(part of this story belongs to Elizabeth Fowler)

'Albert! Time you were up. You start your new job today.'

A low snort with a trace of German accent replied and the duvet moved a little.

The next shout was accompanied by an elbow in the back. 'You know full well the doctor said you need to keep active and your NASA pension isn't enough on its own. You're jolly lucky that Burger World is taking you on. Up, up, get up, Albert.'

'Okay liebling, okay, put the bratwurst on to boil. I'm getting up.'

Standing in his thermal long johns, Albert stared in annoyance at his watch. Relativity be damned, it was only 8 o'clock. He shouted after his wife, 'What's the rush, I can't use my bus pass until after nine thirty?' Albert shuffled his slipper-less feet towards the bathroom, accompanied by muffled German expletives to himself and the cockroach he'd just trodden on.

Once in the kitchen, Albert was faced with an awful shock, 'What is this? Where is my breakfast?'

'You're on a diet Albert, half a bratwurst is all you're getting, doctor's orders to reduce the chance of dementia. And don't you be turning your nose up at the herb tea either. No more coffee for you.'

Albert's face screwed up with displeasure. He popped his breakfast into his mouth in one go and cautiously sniffed the herb tea, which he thought reminiscent of stale Hyena urine. 'Look wife, if I lost half my neurons I'd still be twice as clever as that silly doctor of ours.'

Later, a clean, half starved, bewildered and rather miffed Albert sat on the 21A bus into town. In his hands he clutched his bus pass and a note from his wife, reminding him of where he lived.

Meanwhile, at Burger World, a spotty, presumptuously ambitious nineteen year old manager with two 'O' levels, three if you counted a border line pass in 'text abbreviations for the gifted', took another selfie and paced impatiently by the door, waiting for his new staff to arrive.

'Glad to see you made it in on time Mr Einsdrain, can't have my staff being late on duty,' smirked Carl Minns, new manager of this branch of Burger World. The previous manager having walked out the day before after being caught in the cold store with a female customer in a bizarre and compromising situation. It had been his unlucky day, as head office sent an inspector to the Warley branch to do an assessment of the customer flow that day and he was unimpressed to find the manager missing during the busy lunch hour.

So it was Carl Minns, who introduced Albert to the harassed Roger, who was churning out burgers, chips, and greasy chicken bits in an endless stream from the big fryers and told his job was to add sauces, throw on the salad bits creating a pretend healthy meal and get the results to the serving area fast.

News of the antics of the previous manager had obviously spread and Albert's first morning was busy with gawping customers wanting to view the cold store, while pretending to have come in for a meal. The two waitresses were having a hard time evading the endless stream of smutty suggestions.

All of this went straight past Albert as he plodded on with adding curry sauce, mexican sauce or chilli sauce, all of which appeared identical to him and leaving a trail of dropped bits of sad lettuce, curling cucumber and tomato as he prepared the plates or plastic trays and deposited them on the service area. This was accompanied by a musical libretto echoing from his starving stomach, but he was reassured by the waitresses that he could have a free meal before he left after his lunch time stint. Which cheered him up considerably?

Eventually 3 o'clock came around and an aching, weary Albert piled a plate with chips and burgers with tomato sauce on top and carried it to a small table squashed into a back corner of the kitchens where he could eat. Finishing off with a large plastic mug of coffee he felt much restored and left Burger World with the rest of the afternoon his own. Wandering down Fore Street he passed the library and saw that it was actually open, so he decided to read up on the latest research into Black Holes being done by Brian Cox.

Eventually finding his library card, after offering his 'bus pass' 'B&Q loyalty card' and a 'British Naturalist membership' he didn't know he had, he shuffled to the research section. There selected, The Quantum Universe, Universal Journey through the Cosmos and Private Life of the Atom and finding himself a quiet table settled down to an enjoyable read.

But someone was trying to stop him reading, shaking his arm and talking at him, he looked up and found the Librarian standing over him telling him he would have to go, he really couldn't sleep in the library. Unreasonable woman, Albert thought, as he gathered his notebook, pencil and glasses. She insisted he leave at once and she would put the books away in the morning. Grumbling to himself he walked back into Fore Street and saw it was starting to get dark, better get home, he would certainly be in trouble now.

Somehow, he survived the next few days working at Burger World, his wife was delighted with him and even more so as he said he would stick to her diet and would not eat a big supper when he got home. Just a little sauerkraut, a small potato and mineral water would be fine.

Finding the work was boring but not arduous, Albert might well have carried on, but that was not to be. Possibly as a result of consuming large quantities of hormone treated meat while working at Burger World, Carl was soon displaying worrying tendencies. His pursuit of the waitresses resulted in both resigning in quick succession and it was not long before head office decided that the small Warley branch was more trouble than it was worth and the place was sold to Krafty Chicken.
Albert would probably have to visit the job centre again.

Albert's wife grew increasingly intolerant of him hanging about the house. He'd abandoned the diet she'd designed for him and had developed a predilection for intimate favours about which she had an even greater predilection to avoid like the plague.

'You need to see the doctor again Albert,' she scolded, 'I'm off to stay with my sister in Hamburg for a couple of months.' *'At **least** two months,'* she thought privately. 'You get yourself a job and some medication before I return, they say bromide isn't too bad.'

With his wife gone, Albert raided the freezer and liberated the reserve bratwurst supply, but it didn't give him the same high as one of those, 'Atomic Scrummies' as Burger World called their top of the range snack.

Albert might have been in his eighties, but his biological age was now nearer to his forties. Apart from his desires in life increasing so had his muscles. Probably down to the steroids that were pumped into the cattle along with hormones and antibiotics.

On his visits to the job centre he met up with Roger, Carl and the old manager Harvey, as well as a few other ex Burger World rejects. The Krafty Chicken menu was no match for the burgers they craved. They all had the sweats, convulsions and hallucinations commonly associated with cold Turkey.

Albert had a plan. He formed an alliance with likeminded people, from world leader he became a gang leader. At night they would do the rounds of various burger vans and restaurants rifling through the bins for discarded burger bits which they would reheat at Albert's new flat.

Having cut his hair and with the body of a forty-year-old body builder he'd taken the top flat of a dockside bordello, where he worked part time security for the girls.

Burger World as a business was thriving in most towns and plans to convert the entire land mass of Brazil into a cattle farm were already moving apace. With global warming surprisingly increasing at double the rate, all Burger World restaurants were air conditioned and included screened entertainment. The most popular screening was a live cattle culling in Peru. A board game based on driving cattle to an abattoir proved a great success with the adults and an online game where the players had to make a virtual burger from scratch – including catching the cow, was most popular with the fat and addicted children that waddled through their doors. When a sign writer inadvertently misspelled their name on a major store, Burger World overcame the bad publicity by having him accidentally killed in a Peruvian cattle stampede. It was the second most popular video that Burger World had produced.

Albert took up the study of biology and particularly manipulation of human genetics. He noticed marked differences in the effects of diet. Those who were keen on milkshakes with their burgers were more prone to growing what seemed to be breasts. Often turning transvestite and calling themselves Mabel, or the like. Those who favoured the fizzy drinks tended to have spots and ADHD while the mainly meat eaters became younger and frequent visitors to the rooms below Albert's flat.

Now that Albert was only biologically forty, he had plenty to offer the world. Tomorrow he'd check out the job centre again. Perhaps Carl, alias Caroline, would go with him. Despite the age gap they'd become quite close.

***

The Hitchhiker

Pete hadn't planned on driving far but was certainly going to make the most of a dry sunny day and the pleasurable smooth running of this immaculate classic BMW.

'What a car,' he thought as he settled comfortably into the white leather upholstery and listened to the alluring purr of the three-litre engine at a steady thirty miles per hour, 'absolute luxury.' His eyes keenly surveyed the interior at all the switches, buttons, lights and screens that only God and BMW knew were for.

Suddenly his peripheral vision glimpsed movement in front of the car and Pete instinctively hammered on the brakes, coming to a halt only a breath away from sending some old lady to Valhalla.

Pete pressed the button that opened a window so as to apologise but it was too late, she had already pulled the door open and thrown her walking stick and handbag into the seat well and climbed in after them. 'Thank you young man for stopping, I've been thumbing a lift for ages.'

There didn't seem much Pete could do or say about it now and after all, he owed her something after nearly running her over.

'You need to put your seat belt on.'

'Eh? What's that dear?' she squinted quizzically in his direction.

'Seatbelt!' He shouted, flexing his own to show what he meant.

'Damned new-fangled thing that, how do you work it?' she asked.

Pete leaned across, took the belt and clipped it in place, noticing as he did so that his new passenger smelled of a mixture of peppermint and urine. Still, she wouldn't be in the car for long, what damage could she possibly do?

'Where to then?' Pete enquired.

'Taunton,' came the reply, 'I'm trying to catch my grandson, he's taking our dog to the vet.'

'Taunton?!' Pete looked at his watch then the fuel gauge and back again, both were warning him he'd be on the limits of his ability. Still, if he got on with it the BMW was a fast car and he could just make it back to Bideford in time. He'd just have been away longer than expected . . . that's all.

A short while later and after a few miles with windows open and speeding as fast as he dare, the old lady pointed and screamed, 'there he is, there he is, my grandson with our dog Satan. Oh quick, toot! toot! and stop for him.' Then turning towards Pete with her false teeth loose and a modicum of spittle spray, 'He must have missed the bus, or spent the fare in the bookies. He's a naughty boy that Nathan.'

It was quickly becoming a bad day for Pete, but he felt the guilt of obligation to help this trio of helpless souls, one he'd nearly run over, another a penniless addict and the last, a sick and innocent animal. If he didn't stop, it would look like he was abducting the old lady against her wishes and he was already in enough trouble as it was.

Pete drew the gleaming BMW alongside the boy, who seemed to be an inebriated twenty-fivish thug, and his dog, a large white boxer come mongrel beast, which seemed quite reluctant to be with the boy at all.

'Watcha Gran,' slurred Nathan, using his boot to push the door wide open to the limit of its hinges, throwing Satan on to the back seat and joining him. Safety pins and zips on his jeans noisily scoring the white leather in a most unsightly way.

As Pete now proceeded with even greater hurry towards Taunton, he noticed in the rear-view mirror Nathan emptying his pockets, obviously in search of something urgent. Among the debris were some scraps of paper, betting slips no doubt, a well-used filthy looking cloth, a switch blade and some small plastic bags containing white powder, one of which Satan promptly swallowed without it even touching the sides. Satan's spontaneous eating habits earned him a hefty smack on the head and an earful of choice expletives, some of which Pete had never heard before. It seemed obvious to Pete where the bus fare had gone . . . and no doubt any vet's fee too.

Pete thought to be sociable and asked, 'What's wrong with the dog? Looks fine to me.'

'Na mate, poxy thing has the runs all the time and when not doing that spends its time throwing up. We reckon it's 'cos of what he finds to eat when we let him out at night.'

Satan, by now feeling the effects of the white powder had shoved his head between the front seats and was breathing heavily into Pete's ear while staring vacantly at the road ahead. A foul-smelling drool was hanging from Satan's chops and swaying gently with every bend or bump in the road, that is, until it finally dropped off, on to the handbrake lever.

About the same time as Nathan had asked why on earth Pete was driving them to Taunton when the vet was back there ten miles in Tawstock, Pete had to slow for a sheep loose on the road. As he eased the once pristine BMW past the oblivious sheep, Satan took his chances and leapt through the open window. Shocked by the combined screams from Nathan and his Gran, Pete braked hard and stopped. Nathan was out first having carefully avoided the puréed contents of Satan's bowels that now decorated the back seat along with Nathan's discarded pocket contents. His Gran was next out, her handbag catching in the chrome door handle and ripping it off. 'Stay there,' she yelled.

But Pete accelerated hard and the doors slammed half shut. After a short way down the road he spun the car around to head for home. As he approached his former hitchhikers, he was shocked to see that Satan was on the sheep in a drug crazed frenzy of passion with Nathan's gran beating him mercilessly with her walking stick . . . something the dog appeared to be enjoying.

As Pete approached, Nathan's gran spotted him and realising she now needed a lift home, tried to flag him down. This time Pete wasn't stopping, even if it meant life in prison for manslaughter. Gran's stick was waving him down but succeeded only in hitting the wing mirror and leaving it hanging by a couple of wires, the rubber end of her stick then scored a long black line into the paintwork like a badly done go faster stripe. Pete dared not look in the mirror but if he had, he would have seen Satan throw up, then take a bite out of Nathan's leg before jumping the fence into a field of drug induced dreams – and a whole flock of sheep. Meanwhile Gran was busy flagging down a naïve looking tourist's caravan with French number plates.

Pete drove the car home, not his own home of course but to the chap who collected classic cars and who had let him borrow his prize BMW only that morning for a short trip down the road and back.

Pete hoped he wouldn't be too angry as he was now running much later than expected.

Home too late.

A Winter moonlight cautiously revealed the lonely wasteland of nature's suspicion at his long-awaited homecoming. The tide line of all possibility was already now something long past. His oft treasured anticipation of a warm welcome in his hometown turned to night-time sadness. His ears were met only by the single doleful toll of a faraway church bell. In the empty alleyway, where once stood the cheerful soup kitchen and merry crowd, all was cold and grey as he took his rightful place in a queue of ghosts who'd also left it too late to come home.

***

Karnak revisited.
Beware when you meditate, for the gate opens both ways.

The hour was right, for meditation,
its magic, journeys, and creation.
In Karnak's past, our scene begins,
then by boat, to Vale of Kings.

I see Hatshepsut, by the gate
that leads to ways, that summon fate.
Great queen beside me, in the shade
her mighty temple columns made.

Not there to rule, or give command,
those from the dead, no such demand.
She sits content, in Egypt's sun,
and smiles, as children laugh and run.

We sit as one – but, worlds apart,
yet destiny has blessed each heart.
'Ma' ah salam,' she smiled, then said,
'Now I must leave, to join the dead.'

So friends, my journey is no more,
for I've returned, from mystic shore,
you too can travel, where I've been,
to meet and talk, with pharaoh queen.

'It's a cheap holiday, honest.'

(Two weeks on a French canal -
written from a vague and aging memory)

Background.

By the time the phone call came, I was in my late forties, twice divorced and living on my own in a small bungalow. Before moving in, on one snowy day and following a diesel freezing minus eight night, my new home had stood empty and neglected for three years, which explained the lack of heating and the missing gas meter. Both events duly led to all the pipes freezing up, which is what happened to me too as I attempted to sleep on the cold floor, covered with as much spare clothing as I could find.

I obviously survived to tell the tale and spent the next year making the place habitable and burying my lonely soul in my work. As a fire-fighter, that was easy to do. As part of the fire and rescue service I had also trained in boat handling and even assisted at a local reservoir teaching power boating, mostly with RIBs. (Rigid Inflatable Boats) I had a confidence about my boat skills which was about to be challenged and quite rightly so – because I was wrong, as we shall later see. I mean, how difficult can it be?

The Invitation.

'Hello Richard, it's Joy here, how are you?' Without waiting to find out, she continued, 'we would like you to come on a boating holiday with us . . . in France. It will be very cheap, there will be seven of us and we will buy food in the supermarkets and eat on board. It will be lovely. Bob is going to drive us down in his car. Do say you will come.'

I considered it briefly and being easily led and having nothing better to do . . .also . . . it was good value and cheap, she'd said. I reluctantly agreed.

The journey there.

So, in October, always a good time for an outdoor holiday, 1995, I arrived at their house with my passport, a few clothes in a small bag, my Jo (short oak staff – bit like a broom handle) a book on learning Dutch and something under £200 in cash. I cannot remember exchanging pounds for the then French Franc, but I suppose I did and similarly suppose that I didn't do well out of the swap. At that time of my life I had no idea what a credit card was or even looked like. I had a mortgage and bills to pay.

Climbing into Bob's car were, Joy, her partner Herbert, both in their late fifties and her son, Bob in his early twenties. Somewhere out there in the world were three more people in their own car, making for the same canal boat (read slave ship) on the canal du midi, an often overhung, tree lined, open sewer started long before Napoleon and which connects the Med via another canal to a proper stretch of water - the Atlantic.

Remember the bit about, 'it's really cheap'? We boarded our ferry at Poole and took the eight-hour night boat to St Malo.

The ferry was posh! When I say posh, I mean it. I had a double cabin all to myself, with a window! Not only was there a well-stocked drinks fridge but a large bowl of fruit . . . real fruit and a large bunch of fresh flowers too. 'All this for me?' I thought!

The dream holiday had begun well, with the nightmare yet to arrive.

'Ah, Richard,' came a voice with a knock on the door, 'we're going to have a meal in the restaurant, will you join us?' Well, as I was always a keen eater, it sounded good - until I saw the menu, or more pertinently the prices down the right-hand side. Dinner – one course – was £17.90, the equivalent of £32.50 some twenty years later. As I had less than 200 quid for the fortnight, at that rate I'd be broke by the following Monday. That's the trouble with a posh boat, I mean, whatever happened to the Smörgåsbord for a fiver, so I declined and ate the free biscuits and bananas in my cabin. The voyage was reasonably comfortable except that the floor spent a long time in and out of the horizontal. At one point I looked out of my cabin door to see lifejackets had been pre-emptively strung up outside cabin doors along the length of the corridor.

After that it was a 620 mile non-stop drive to the south of France. Now, bearing in mind that we were in a car capable of 130 mph and Bob only operated at two levels, full throttle or, at a glimpse of anything resembling a police car, stationary. Our journey took closer to six hours than the predicted ten and even closer to death I suspect at times. We did make a brief roadside stop to examine the packed sandwiches in the cool box. I say 'examine' advisedly because the cooling slime, which at one time was sealed in its toxic proof container, had escaped. After wiping off the said sticky slime (of unknown toxicity) from the sandwiches, which to be fair, were wrapped in thin plastic film, we cautiously ate a few; each person waiting for any suspicious sudden spasms to appear in fellow travellers. Bob's driving was evidently instrumental in all passengers staying conversation free: all otherwise hell bent on deep silent prayer for the duration.

Arrival at the boat yard.

Somehow, we found the boatyard and met up with our fellow adventurers, Ruth and Rupert, about the same age as Joy and Herbert, none of them married but all just very good friends, and Dave, another young bloke of Bob's age. They all seemed like nice people and obviously knew each other, after all, why go on a canal boat for two weeks with people you consider a touch iffy?

Someone had to sign up to be the Captain of the vessel we were hiring. By unanimous decision I proudly and foolishly accepted the nomination. The girl in the office took my passport, muttered instructions in French and made me sign a document, also in French. It was only hindsight that saw my popularity as captain as a way of placing all responsibility for any loss or sinking of the said vessel in someone else's court – mine!

Captain Naivety at the wheel with a cheap beer.

 Captain Naivety was shown the rudiments of the boat and the few controls with which it was fitted, steering wheel, throttle and gear lever, (just in case reversing was ever needed.) It was very basic training – 'here eez boat. . . there eez water, bon jour.'

*Plastic swimming pool tub with lid -
called a canal boat in France.*

The crew clambered aboard with their suitcases and disappointed expressions, as the boat obviously didn't fit the grandiose image in their minds nor the photographic machinations of the French brochure. Still, they quickly occupied their chosen cabins, Joy and Herbert having the best. At the end of which manoeuvrings, it was obvious there were none left for me. But, hey, 'you can have the captain's cabin, there is a useful long bench with cushions, and it has lovely windows on three sides and you'll always be close to the steering wheel.' To be honest, it wasn't a bad idea, it was the largest, most airy room on the boat, and the only one above the water line.

The boat was interesting, it was made of fibre glass and the hull served either of two purposes, one as the hull of a canal boat or two, when settled into a hole in someone's garden, a swimming pool. Hence the beast appeared boat shaped from above the water and swimming pool shaped beneath it.

Before setting off, it was decided by a committee, that didn't include me, that a visit to the supermarket for supplies was in order. I handed over a large wad of requested cash, may have been forty quid I reckon, after all, that was the plan. They bought food in the supermarket, cooked it on board and all was going to be well . . . and cheap. After a while the shoppers returned with the goods. It was at that point I realised their idea of food was a lot different to mine. The shopping was proudly withdrawn from the bags with a flourish, three bottles of red wine, a vast amount of Revolting Pate, (that's probably exactly what it said in French on the packet) and some other unmentionable crappy things that I couldn't eat without throwing up. So, I'm starving, even shorter on my limited funds, solely responsible for this very expensive boat (I'm sure the French will say it is anyway, even if just a cheap swimming pool with a lid and a motor), I sleep in the main thoroughfare come wheel house and kitchen of said boat and I can't go home for two weeks. What can go wrong eh? How difficult could it be?

Why didn't it respond to the controls?

I had wrongly assumed (yes, dangerous word that) steering would be the same as on a RIB. Propeller at the back and steering wheel at the front – the two somehow linked between. With a RIB you can drive at an angle really fast towards the bank then at an appropriately judged moment, drop the revs, go through neutral, turn the wheel hard to steer towards bank and throw it into reverse with a good burst of power. It is a magical manoeuvre that brings the boat in parallel to and touching the bank at a dead stop. Perfect. I couldn't understand why my bathtub canal boat didn't respond in the same way and I made several attempts before aborting the idea altogether. The answer by the way is down to the propeller, on the canal boat it stayed in one plane and only turned round, on the RIB the whole thing moves, so power and steering go together and there's no rudder. Moving away from the canal bank could also be interesting. If you steered too quickly towards the centre of the canal all that happened was you scraped the back of the boat along the bank for fifty yards or so.

They did vote for me as Captain so they must have thought I knew what I was doing. No idea when or if they discovered differently.

South to Sete on the Med.

We chugged along the canal in our little boat. As captain dogsbody and brim full of confidence with my skills on outboard powered vessels, I ran her flat out – which I think might have been just over six knots. I'm no longer positive about the speed the moped sized engine could give us. The engine also heated the water tank on board. That hot water was to get us all in the same stuff, metaphorically speaking. Joy dictated that no one used hot water after we had moored and the engine stopped, because she liked a morning shower and the tank must remain warm all night for her to do so. I might just point out that the tank held just enough water for one shower. I managed to have two showers during my fortnight and both occurred when we moored for rare stops at marinas with facilities. The hot water question laid down a marker for later seething hostile events that eventually led to mutiny. But we haven't arrived at Sete yet – and it looked as if we never would when the engine conked out some ten miles from our host marina. As the noise of the diesel moped engine signified its untimely death by not breathing anymore, I managed to steer closer to shore as a dwindling momentum slowly edged our boat forward. There was much kafuffle and annoyance that the boat was smaller than they thought it should be and now failed to travel as far as they thought it should go. The engine refused to respond to commands. Herbert sprang into action, about the only action I saw from him in two whole weeks, he was going ashore to make a phone call to the boatyard and sort them out. Well, he did make shore but only after stepping into the gap between boat and terra firma. In some ways this was useful as I could now clearly see how deep the murky water was – about waist height near the bank I should say. He did not look a happy bunny.

It wasn't long before his telephone encounter with, quite likely highly amused French boat owners, was terminated with the knowledge that running the engine flat out overheats it and it cuts out automatically until cooled again. They probably told me that in French at the boat yard, or was that what was printed on the notice above the still glowing, red warning light? Who knows? However, we were soon mobile again and most of us had remained dry, a blessing indeed.

My guess is that we stopped for the night somewhere along the bank and as nothing has been found in the memory vault, I can only assume it was uneventful. Either that or it was so bad my neurons refuse to revisit the trauma.

Next clear memory is of a circular lock with four exits and watching some German tourists go around in circles trying to steer a reluctant plastic tugboat style vessel towards their chosen exit. The toy-like looking tugboat must have previously endured frightful experiences on that part of the canal and it was at least twenty minutes before it obeyed orders and moved off into the unknown to experience more of them. Intriguingly our canal crossed a river, the river flow being stopped to allow canal traffic to pass, before returning to its course. The steady rain that was falling and the wind that was beginning to blow were of little significance to us at this point. Talking of pointing, at no time did anyone local offer advice or share warnings of impending doom. It must have been amusing for experienced canal users to watch a group of ignorant Britishers embarking on a route of no return, just as we too had a laugh at the expense of the hapless Germans on the tugboat.

Our boat was soon upon the high seas, well almost, we were on a huge pond called the etang de thau, some twenty kilometres long (13 miles for us imperialist die hards) and Sete was at the far end and was our stop for the night. All we had to do was get there. I have no recollection how we navigated, but my best guess is we had some sort of map; well someone onboard had a map because it wasn't the captain for sure. We steered past mile after mile of posts indicating vast oyster beds, until with a stroke of luck; we found the marina at Sete before dark.

Oh, you remember the 'cook on board, it will be cheap,' bit? Well they had decided to eat out in a restaurant using one of those plastic cards I'd never seen before. I was in luck; I was treated to a meal. I don't want to appear ungrateful and I cannot remember what I ate but you can bet it was some sort of sea creature and a salad. For God's sake, where's the steak and ale pie and chips?

Now something else happened that night. The weather took a turn for the worse and a decent wind blew up along the length of the Etang and straight at Sete. A head wind loomed for our return journey on the morrow. That was enough to cause a mass desertion of our noble craft. The two women, Rupert and young Bob opted to take the train back to somewhere unknown to me, both then and now, but, as the boat cannot be abandoned in Sete, Herbert, young Dave and I would motor across the Etang to rejoin the canal.

By morning the weather had worsened but we set out hopefully – hopefully not to drown. The boat did not have lifejackets, communications, flares or first aid, but it did have an engine that liked to cut out if you made it work too hard. Rolling waves were all topped by white horses which at times galloped over the front of our vessel with a mighty thump and were more like cart horses. I was beginning to enjoy this, now **this** was a holiday, excitement, adventure, the stuff of life (and death) it was like my work in the fire brigade, a dedicated team facing hardship together, overcoming all odds to win the day. Unfortunately, my team didn't see it quite that way and young Dave practised his expletive vocabulary with every lurch of the boat or pounding by a wave. Herbert wasn't much better and kept on about us making for port and safety.

Why on earth would we do that while we're having such fun?

After about five miles we were passing the small port of Meze on our starboard side. To prevent young Dave from apoplexy I agreed with Herbert's demand we run for shelter but knew all too well that once we were in port we would not be able to leave again and continue to the canal. Wind speed exceeded our boat speed and we'd just plod into the wind and wave until we ran out of fuel, the engine failed, or we sank. It was game over.

A flat-bottomed canal boat is no match for rolling waves nor does it, without a keel, hold its position in the water when you want to steer. I was struggling to turn her around in the small harbour, it didn't matter which direction we wanted to go, the wind blew it towards land, but not the bit we wanted. I expressed a doubt that I could make it to the mooring. This was Herbert's singular chance to display his own extensive canal boat skills and he took command of the wheel but unfortunately not of the boat which had ideas of its own. We made a large circle, which would have been much bigger if it wasn't for the fine white anchored yacht that blocked our way. There was an almighty cracking noise, which could have been heard in Dover, as our little canal boat was deflected in the direction of a mooring. Herbert pretended not to notice what he'd done. I wondered which of us had come off worse, the ten-franc canal boat or the million-dollar yacht.

We tied up and prepared for the night. Now, if the yacht hadn't damaged us, the constant bumping of the hull all night against the concrete quayside must have. I was grateful for sleeping as best I could above the water level and next to the door onto deck and then safety on shore. In the early hours I left the boat and sat on the harbour wall with feet dangling towards the surprisingly warm breeze. I sat there for a while just enjoying the moment. They do say that it is feelings that abide longest in the body and not thoughts. Certainly, that is true of that day.

Morning came and so began the habit of buying fresh bread and occasional croissants each day. I think I bought these ones as I remember walking along the quayside. When I returned the rest of the crew had arrived from wherever they had been. They had arrived in two cars, because they had news. Good news and bad news.

The new boat.

The bad news was that heavy rains had put the river into flood, and they could no longer close the lock gates to allow canal traffic through. So, the sort of bad news was that we couldn't sail our boat back to the canal, which if you remember was the purpose of the holiday. The good news however was that the boat yard had sanctioned a new vessel for us, and we were at liberty to abandon ship in Meze. We loaded whatever we had with us into the two cars and made for the boat yard to be united with our new canal ship. Compared to the swimming pool tub of earlier days our new vessel was like a battleship, bristling with cabins of all sizes and this time, there was one for me!

I suspect that this was more like the boats in the brochures but, once you had burdened yourself with a thousand miles of misery and hardship to get there; it was quite easy to be fobbed off with the inferior tub.

Joy chose a cabin for me, 'I've given you a super cabin to yourself, plenty of room and a sky light too, right at the front of the boat, lovely.'

It wasn't quite how I saw it, Joy was using estate agent speak, I suspect.

True, it was roomy, but not in height, also the pointed shape of the bow meant the cabin tapered at one end. The bed had an ill at ease curved shape to fit the hull and the skylight? Well, previous sailors, not using the aforesaid cabin, had left the damn thing open in the rain and the carpet was wet. Worse still, it had been wet long enough for mould and bacteria to get a good grip and it smelled awful - That dreadful smell of a damp rag that's been left in a dark cupboard for too long. Still, it was home for the next week or so and I could always breathe clean air while we were moored or while I steered.

No one else wanted the privilege of steering; they seemed to prefer lounging in the plastic chairs on the upper deck and drinking wine. This boat was higher out of the water than the other one and combined with the branches of overhanging trees that lined the canal it led to some interesting events. We once saw one boat lose everything off the top deck to a tree and I inadvertently came too close to a branch which nearly swept our own chairs into the canal, much to the annoyance of Herbert who was sitting in one at the time. Strewth, did he shout! Had he been below in the cabin, steering or cooking it wouldn't have happened. Later we were to see some hapless crew on another boat lose their bicycles overboard, where they would join tons of other rubbish snuggled in enduring centuries of old French mud. We also watched a desperate family try to recover their washing line and clothes that had got hung up on some tenacious French brambles that adorned an overhanging tree.

I kept my skylight open when the sun was shining and when on the move. I suspect that the awful smell drifted from the bowels of the for'ard end and permeated other parts of the vessel. After a couple of days Joy took pity on me and sorted out the smelly cabin I had – she lifted the carpet and threw it overboard where it conveniently sank! Everything seemed to go in the canal, including the sewage from canal boats. The French were obviously adopting a simpler system than collecting sewage, processing it and then putting it into the canal. Removing the middleman was much cheaper. Cheap holidays were attractive to some and always to the gullible.

*As captain gullible, I chose my own dress code, an old fire brigade
flat cap because it felt more like a U boat captain's hat,
and a pair of shorts I'd made myself ...
by cutting off the legs of a pair of jeans.*

Lock gates made for interesting distractions.

The lock gates were always operated by a lock keeper,
often they lived in pleasant houses with lawns down to the
water. On occasion, a dog or a cockerel would patrol the
bank, ensuring nervous people stayed on board. Our new
boat, designed on a scale model of the *Bismark*, had a slight
over-hang where the hull met the superstructure. Before I
explain the relevance of this fact, I'd like you to know what
had happened with the crew. They had fallen out with each
other! They had split into two groups of three with me as a
neutral. Up to this point, when they weren't eating ashore,
the two ladies were taking it in turns to cook. Remember?
Cheap holiday, buy in supermarkets, cook on board! As
their disagreements escalated into a walk-the-plank level
mutiny, I feared the worst of a boat captain's nightmares –
no dinners. And I didn't have one of those magic plastic

cards that appeared to secure free dinners everywhere you went.

On this fateful day, as we slowly motored into a water filled lock, a huge saucepan of chilli-con-carne sat ready on the cooker. No one had spoken as to when we might eat. In fact, no one was speaking. I feared I might not eat again for days, a terrible thought. Some of the crew went ashore to hold the mooring lines; an obligatory routine as the French like to open the gates very quickly so as to damage your boat, particularly they gifted this experience to British tourists – a bit like Disney land rides but with real chances of drowning – much more fun.

The lock gates were closed behind us and the water level began to drop - but our boat didn't. Yes, you'll have worked it out yourselves, won't you? The damn boat was hung up on the overhanging lip I wrote of earlier. One side of our Titanic was by then a metre below the other and the deck tilting at an alarmingly increasing rate . . . probably much to the amusement of the lock keeper . . . perhaps he didn't have a telly, perhaps he didn't need one with the sort of daily entertainment he could have with novice canal boaters. The remnants of my on-board crew screamed in panic and harmonised with the screams of those on shore, all loud enough to obscure the laughter from the keeper, his family and his dog.

I ignored the desperate calls to abandon ship – I was not only the captain, but I was hungry too. As the remaining crew clawed and scrambled their way ashore, like the ancient mariner, I was alone. My sole purpose on board was to save the dinner which was in danger of sliding to a premature doom off the cooker surface. Two eager hands of one mind took the saucepan and placed it safely in the sink, where it could slide no further. At this point, the boat slipped off the concrete edge and righted itself with a mighty thump and splash. I and the chilli were safe. The shock of near death in a French canal lock brought a momentary truce and later that day, the chilli was to meet a much more satisfying and nobler end.

Each lock gate brought a new adventure, particularly the Nine Locks of Beziers, (*think, the trials of Hercules*) where the keepers to save time and water would open two compartments at once. To supplement a meagre income they probably sold tickets for people to watch the fun - The fun of seeing one man sitting on deck holding a rope while four tons of water a minute attempted to drive his pathetic boat against the lower gates. These locks were so deep that they had poles fitted in the walls so you could slide the restraining ropes down them. Ropes weren't long enough to reach the lock bank above and it would have been suicidal to try.

On one such deep lock, I sat on the fore deck holding the rope which would keep our boat in place. The French lock keeper, probably hoping for some good camera footage or being a descendant of someone killed at Agincourt, opened the sluices as quickly as he could. A wall of frenzied white water rushed at our floating home and began to push it further in to the lock. I was no lightweight nor was I weak, so I took a good grip and strained my back to hold us against the surge. I quickly realised that my strength wasn't going to hold out – I could see the boat slipping backwards leaving me still holding the rope and doing a bit of white-water surfing. I took a quick turn of the rope around the fancy chrome deck railings to give me some assistance. I watched as the railings took the strain and began to lean. I half expected the screws to ping out one by one and the railings go overboard. Fortunately, we survived intact, but it was a somewhat interesting experience. The lock keeper went off to his hut for another bottle of *Napoleon's Blood* red wine and to carve another notch on the back of the door.

The French probably organise bus and coach trips to the nine locks for the general populace to watch the foolhardy canal boaters attempt the rapids. It has a similar ethos to Roman gladiators or the Spanish bullfighters – someone might die.

It was a sunny day when we moored quayside at the top of the locks. I played some simple tunes on a mouth organ and looked across the countryside. I remember there was a young couple sitting on the boat in front of me and a sense of loneliness washed over me. Everybody else had gone exploring, what, I don't know. I was enamoured of a Dutch girl at the time, so I sometimes thought of her. I was attempting to learn Dutch. If you want my advice, don't bother, as they all speak perfect English.

Carcasonne.

At Carcasonne, our merry band was unbelievably still together. Despite the time of year, it was warm in the evening and I walked up into the medieval citadel with

Ruth, Rupert and Dave. I think we had a coffee in a café next a cobbled square dominated by a huge tree. Someone played the guitar nearby. It was a pleasant visit, soon over, and we returned to the boat which at times resembled a slave ship . . . in a nice way of course. When moored and convenient, i.e. out of public gaze, I would practise with the Japanese short staff on the bank. A sort of meditative event in that my mind was only on that practise. . . and the next dinner of course.

Carcasonne was a turning point – we needed enough time to return the *Bismark* to its home port – preferably intact. The crew's minds were taken not only by the scenery but by how much they didn't like each other. It was still a one shower a day boat and not a luxury that was taken in turns. I might have been captain of the vessel, but Joy was definitely in charge.

The nights passed quietly enough and invariably it was me that steered our vessel during the day. Each morning it was someone's turn to be up first and wander the French countryside in search of a bakery. They love their bread, do the French, but I can't say it seemed that wonderful to me. Still, duty calls.

One morning as the sun cleared the mist, it was Rupert's turn.

Ruth and Dave went with him, perhaps to discuss mutiny or perhaps afraid to be outnumbered aboard ship. Anyway, they seemed to be gone for hours, we should have had breakfast (that's what the French call a lump of bread) and been on our way. Eventually they returned, apparently, they'd taken a wrong turn in the countryside and become lost. It had been a traumatic marathon struggle to find the canal and our boat again. Rupert sat on the bank some distance away down the tow path, staring at the water through his fingers. Ruth and Dave came aboard with that luxurious of all breakfasts – the bread. They explained about being lost and that Rupert was taking it rather badly and wouldn't come aboard. Now that's not a lot of use if your way home is by boat. I went to see if I could offer words of some comfort to him, while I suspect Joy and Herbert were enjoying his impending suicide. Rupert wasn't up to talking much – he'd had it. Burnt out and drowning in the misery of perhaps not so much having been lost but that he'd actually found the cursed boat again.

Eventually he came aboard and said, 'we're getting off at the next stop where there's a railway, we're going home.'

That was a sad moment, but a greater shock was to come, for Joy proclaimed, 'You needn't bother, our cases are already packed.'

I mulled over the implications of this conflict. I came with Joy in Bob's car and have no ferry ticket of my own. I have very little money left of the very little I had to start with. I am the responsible person for this expensive boat and liable for any loss– six months in a French prison would make me late for work. (Bear in mind this was our second boat, the first having been damaged and also abandoned.) A canal boat on such an unfriendly canal cannot be managed by one person alone and there would be no one on board to cook. A French prison was beginning to look a more attractive option.

The departure.

I don't recall the name of the town, but we had left the nine locks behind us. As we moored up, the evening dusk lurked in ambush in the time-honoured way of revolutionary French dusk. It wasn't too far to walk into town and the chemin de fer and its gare. I went with them, carrying a case and speaking in friendly and conciliatory terms. The evening air was warm, and they seemed happy enough to be leaving. Still no doubt they would have photos and fond memories of their canal holiday and tales to tell – until their dying days.

Three down, four left – I hoped!

Joy, Herbert and Bob were indeed still on board celebrating when I returned from the railway station. The next day we continued our merry bread eating way back to the home boat yard. We had a rare stop at a marina on the way, where I enjoyed my second shower of the holiday.

The trip home.

The boat yard was pleased to have their boat back. They didn't notice the carpet was missing. It was another night of the cheap as chips holiday where Joy and Herbert decided to eat out again – probably on the money they saved by talking me into making up the numbers. Perhaps it was a group discount – "eef you ave more zan seex personnes, then deux go free, tres bonne n'est pas?"

As I was almost broke and a bit peeved about all the food we had on board and which still remained uneaten on our last night, I opted to stay at home and knock something up myself. Probably better than anything the French were supplying on shore, I fried up a great heap of sliced potatoes and ate them with an equally large heap of those small pickled gherkin things. I can tell you, it was a fine meal . . . and very cheap, as promised.

The journey back to St Malo was endured in the same manner as the trip from St Malo … with the driver in fear of the French police and the rest of us in fear of our lives. Joy and Herbert did speak on route of some delightful but well-hidden café only they knew of in some remote village – about which I was just as remote in my interest. 'Who cares,' I thought, looking forward to blighty and some proper food.

The ferry on the way home was very different, now we'd spent all our money in France there was no point in a lavish vessel to take us home. We were broke and of no more value to the French economy.
The cabin was as simple as they could build and the idea of fresh fruit, flowers and a drinks cabinet merely a distant memory to savour.

On arrival at Joy's home they unloaded from Bob's car; two full black dustbin bags of food in various states of decay. "Would you like to take some of this home with you," Joy asked, "there's rather a lot of it?"
Well you know what? We should have eaten the bloody stuff in France, not brought it home, whatever it was – probably some left over bread and several kilos of pate and salmonella – fully energised after a trip in a warm car. I declined their kind offer and, as they despondently carried their unwanted burden to the house, I bade them goodbye and set off for home, some chips and a bath.

Captain Wary, late of the canal du midi.

Leroy.

Leroy tried to relax in the tiny car that had been written into the story for him, he wasn't angry, nor did he have any hate in him – but he was once more disappointed. Mavis Bagcroft, the so-called author and now calling herself Kitty Hurricane to enhance her image, was a bigoted trollop. Leroy was a kindly man always trusting and generous and now he was Mavis' ex-boyfriend. Trusting he was, until he found out she was sleeping around – around most of the publishing companies. She'd proved so popular that even provincial publishers with a one room office and computers still running on XP, were phoning her up to see if they could do business.

Finally, some top publisher, fearing unwanted exposure and not the sort he'd enjoyed with Mavis, decided to buy her off by publishing a complete set of her books. Sadly, Leroy appeared in most of them and always in a bad light, he was sick of it and put the word out on the street that he needed to hire an author from the dark side to put Mavis to bed. Not in the way you might think but in the time-honoured way of the printing industry.

Leroy desperately needed to recover his life as a medical student and be reinstated in his volunteer work for the homeless. He turned in desperation to the Cosa Nostra author's association, based in Sicily and they provided a research team. Although at first, they offered a sniper, saying it was quicker and cheaper. They soon discovered that not only was Kitty Hurricane's name false but so was much of her biography. She had indeed gone to a private school but proving intellectually inadequate, the school sent her back home with a full refund after only three weeks of the first term. Her parents were not nobility as she claimed, though they did live in a grand country manor. Her father was a common man working as an accountant for a charity, with a few jobs for pensioners on the side. He and his lady of the night wife lived in luxury far beyond his declared earnings.

Cosa Nostra of Sicily offered to have the pair 'rubbed out' at a discounted price as Leroy was an existing customer. But all Leroy wanted was his own life back and not to be ridiculed in public by a vindictive half witted, ill-educated and vengeful trollop like Mavis. God, how he regretted befriending her that night in the rain when her car broke down, he should have known better. It did make him wonder why she was as scantily dressed as she was while hanging about outside the army barracks.

So, dear friends, we come to the end of our tale and the advice we wish to share.

Don't give such appalling writing the opportunity to be promoted in public. The likes of Kitty Hurricane abound in the publishing business, don't be taken in. Even when condemning it, you feed the wolf of publicity. Take heed. You don't want a visit from Sicily, do you?

***

"Virus – what virus?"

Retired road sweeper, Fred Bloggs, had won the lottery big time and it gave him the chance to buy a beautiful Georgian mansion with its own grounds, lake, stables and servants. It also found him a wife - or rather she found him. She didn't much care for the name Bloggs though as it seemed overly common for a lady of her station – a new station that is, her old one being Euston – so she called herself Lady Marjoram Phorbes. Yes, you did read that right. Mabel, her real name, wasn't that bright. However, she was quite attractive for someone approximately forty and Fred was an easy-going type. He liked his beer and telly, and my goodness what a telly he had bought himself, more like a cinema screen. He had hoped to start his own beer brewing kit too until his wife put a stop to it, saying that it would make the house smell funny.

Fred was watching a report on the rising death tolls with the new Covid 19 virus on the TV, when his wife stood in front of him and said, 'what a load of rubbish you watch, I'm off out, the roads are clear at the moment and I'm taking the Jag into town. There's a nice dress in M&S and they're open because they sell food. I won't be long, unless I find a wine bar open afterwards. And do stop dropping crisps down the back of my new sofa!'

'You shouldn't be going out on non-essential journeys, the government wan ….'

'Stuff the government, what do they know about anything. If you were less dopey, you'd realise that.' She shoved Fred's credit card into her purse and left for the car in one of her moods.

Fred turned the TV off and wandered towards the kitchen to see what cook was preparing for tea. Through the window he heard the double crump of a nearby shotgun and a shout from his gamekeeper of 'got you, you beauty.'

'Could be pheasant next week for dinner with luck,' thought Fred, 'or perhaps we'll have some trout from the lake.' He reminded himself to check with the head gardener on how the walled vegetable garden was progressing with fresh produce. They were quite self-sufficient at the mansion, they even had their own spring and a backup electricity generator, the staff all lived on site. It was an oasis of security against the killer virus and yet his wife was out there putting all their lives at risk …. For a dress! She'd have nowhere to hang it anyway as all her wardrobes were packed to the gunnels.

Fred never noticed that his wife hadn't returned home that night. They were to have separate rooms once married as she'd told him that's what posh people do. She had only slept with him before she persuaded him to tie the knot, but after that, she somehow seemed to lose interest. He'd tried the interconnecting door a few times, but it seemed stuck. 'One day,' he thought, 'I'll have the handyman take the door off and fix it.' Breakfast came and went, as did lunch and dinner and still no sign of the Jag and its belligerent driver. Fred was watching a replay of Chelsea against some foreign team when the maid came in and said, 'telephone for you sir, it's the police. Will you take it here or in the library?'

Pressing pause on the TV remote, Fred smiled and said, 'I'll take it here dear, thank you.'

'Fred Bloggs speaking, can I help you?'

There was a momentary pause at the other end, then a questioning voice answered. 'I'm so sorry sir I was trying to contact Mr Phorbes, it's important sir, city police matter.'

'Phorbes is my wife's chosen name officer, I am her husband god help me, has she been speeding again?'

'I'm afraid it is much worse than that sir, can I ask you to sit down. We would normally call around and speak perso....'

'Yes, yes, officer I understand, we are all self-isolating here, it was only that my wife felt there was something essential she had to fetch from town, please carry on officer.'

'Ah yes, she managed to buy the item sir, a rather fetching red dress which she was wearing when we stopped her for the third time today for taking unnecessary journeys. She was a little unlucky with the last officer, he was one of those who had been happily retired and was drafted back in. They said if he didn't, he would lose some of his pension ... then they stuck him on a 12-hour shift in a busy part of town. Trouble is she looked down on him, blew cigarette smoke in his face, called him a pleb and a servant of the people and didn't he know who she was etc. Well as he'd only got a few minutes of shift left before he could go back for his first meal of the day at the temporary police hostel tent, he arrested her and called for armed backup and the van. Your car is safe sir, it's in the police pound, it'll be fifty quid to release it but as it's not an essential journey sir I'd leave it there. They're doing a discounted storage rate of a tenner a day while the emergency is on, can't say fairer than that eh sir?

Fred fiddled impatiently with the remote, the screen was freeze-framed just before it looked like his team might score, 'so what about my wife then officer, what have you done with her now?'

'Ah, I was coming to that sir, it's why I called. The desk sergeant was not best pleased when she turned up in front of him, all red faced, and coughing like a good 'un, she was. She is now in the local hospital … you can't visit her sir it's all quarantine. Because of her, we've now lost three officers from custody, the custody sergeant, the custody suite, a police dog and two vehicles for isolation and deep clean. The superintendent is hopping mad, because he'd been on duty all day and wanted to go home to be with his new wife, now he'll be sorting this all night instead. He was going to throw the book at her … could have got her two to three years I reckon but the doctor said not to waste time as the prognosis was not favourable.'

Fred was a simple man of few words and none of them as long as those just used by the officer. 'In plain English officer, what does that mean please?'

'Afraid that's the bad news I 'm calling about sir, I'm afraid she may not make the morning. The hospital will keep you informed. Don't worry about prosecution sir, we've dropped all charges, you won't hear from us again. Have a good evening sir.'

The phone clicked dead. Fred handed it back to the maid, who always enjoyed listening in, 'thanks dear, can you let cook know we probably will be permanently one less for meals … oh and ask her nicely if she'd knock up a few chips for me … oh and a bottle of beer … that corona one will do. No need for a glass.' Fred flicked the play button and in a few moments the household knew that Chelsea had scored. 'Yes, yes, yes, yahoo!'

Lady Marjoram Phorbes nee Mabel Smith, formally of flat 2a Calcutta Square Euston passed away in the early hours and was despatched according to new government rules on mass cremations. Like all the others too, she wore a fetching black numbered body bag in place of the essential red dress.

Fred Bloggs survived the entire emergency by staying in isolation with all the happy well-fed staff. He eventually married the cook, who said she like sleeping with him and he could have beer and chips anytime he liked.

***

Reggie and Betty's stay in America

Betty had always wanted to visit the land of the free and the home of the brave. Now, there she was, and having a good close-up view of their interesting legal system.
It had started reasonably well. The flight had been pleasant enough  until Reggie had a couple of bouts of air sickness and a panic attack about the type of aircraft they were on . . . a new Boeing 737 max jetliner or something. Must have been a good plane though because he said it had been in the news a lot lately. Poor old Reggie's sparsely distributed luck abandoned him again at LA airport, his case must have brushed against a drug smuggler's luggage and become contaminated. Betty took photos of the drug dog playing with its toy while Reggie was tazered and handcuffed; all a bit of a shock for an arthritic seventy-year-old with a pacemaker and who now twitches uncontrollably whenever he sees a pair of rubber gloves. Still, those nice policemen gave them both a coffee each and

shared selfies with them as they were released via a service exit.

It was still pleasantly warm outside despite it now being two am. There was only one taxi left at the rank, so they availed themselves of both it and the driver's advice for a hotel. They had missed their connecting sleeper train and would need to rearrange for the following day.

The fact that the new train ticket cost them twice as much as the earlier booking with no refund from the missed trip, seemed quite inconsequential after the trauma of their disturbing night at Hotel Cukaracha (Hotel Cockroach). The hotel was frequented by the local ladies of the night, was a transit camp for asylum seekers, breakfast looked like it was a warmed up meal deal from the bin of a neighbouring Macdoodles and they'd spent a sleepless night on rubber sheets scratching at whatever small creatures infested the darkness.

The same smiling taxi driver took them to the station via a lengthy scenic route, as he explained, 'we have loadsa time before youra traina leaves.' They arrived at the huge station with a minute to spare, losing one suitcase in the process of boarding. Not to worry though as it was the one the drug dog had taken a fancy to and they wanted no repeat of such holiday trauma.

The general plan was to travel north to Seattle, because Betty had liked the film of the same name, then go south east to Missouri, because an old neighbour had a friend who once lived there. Disturbingly they were now playing it by ear, because they simply hadn't realised just how big a place the states were.

They made it to Seattle but it didn't look like anything from Betty's film, still, they visited where the native Indians had once long ago lived happily for 4,000 years and the bare land where forests once flourished before the logging industry took over. Their guide, cheap at $40 an hour, (I mean a dollar is only about 20 pence isn't it?) took them to a back street parking lot where she showed them a home-made plaque, commemorating the foolhardy bravery of some executed English patriot in the glorious war for Independence. They would have been mugged in the nearby street but for the fact they had no money on them and looked like they had suffered enough already. On only day four, Reggie made a rare decision, based partly on his own over confidence and general dislike for what he'd already endured in America. He decided to take charge and hire his own car and drive to the places on Betty's list. What could possibly go wrong eh?

The still jet lagged and traumatised Reggie was high on vitamin pills and strong coffee when he hired his vehicle, the fact that it was a pickup truck with a seemingly innocuous 'all skunks and democrats should be shot' on the rear screen, did not seem to bother him. It was cheap and comfortable to sit in and Betty was quite pleased because a truck like this was in a film she liked with Bronson, or was it Heston? McQueen? Well someone famous anyway.

Thanks to the wide, well maintained roads, Reggie found that driving an automatic wasn't so bad after all and after a few hundred miles he became used to vehicles passing him on both sides. Although the occasional tooting and rude gesturing from some drivers was a little annoying and at least twice, Betty had to reprimand him for trying to return them. 'Hands on the wheel Reggie, hands on the wheel and watch the road,' she'd say, then get back to studying her new Californian cookbook, the pages on variants of hash brownies were already well thumbed.

Reggie was pleased they were on a major road because he was totally confused by the way Americans used four-way crossings, it seemed so odd that first there had priority regardless of direction of travel. He had also been glad of the pickup's good brakes. They had proved very useful.

After about a thousand miles, three tank fills and an earlier giant all-day breakfast, seemingly cooked for a family of eight, Betty screamed out loud, 'here, here, turn off here.'

'Where, where?' he shouted back.

'There, there,' she screamed pointing to a small turnoff leading to an even smaller road, 'it's Sundance, Wyoming. It will be like the film, Botch Cassidy and the Sundance Kiss. Oooh, it's so exciting. . . . mind that car Reggie, he's on the wrong side of the road. Yankee idiot!' she screamed out of her car window, trying her best to emulate her newly learned American gestures.

A few tense miles down the narrow road and Betty had recovered her composure, when she noticed something.

'Reggie, I think they want you to stop.'

'Who does?

'**They** do. The police behind us with blue lights and waving at us.'

Reggie did what he would have done at home, pulled in to let them pass, after all it couldn't be **him** they wanted, could it?

Well they didn't pass, they just parked up behind him, now with all sirens in full wail mode. Two heavily built (a polite euphemism on the author's part) officers of the law both pointing some sort of weapons in his direction, approached Reggie's pickup, screaming, 'Show us your hands, show us your hands.'

'What did they say dear?' Reggie asked his wife.

'They said you should wear those damned hearing aids for once!' she yelled, now eyeball to eyeball with her annoyingly too often deaf husband.

As Reggie took his foot off the brake pedal the automatic gearbox decided to do what they always do, the pickup crept forward. This incensed the officers even more . . . it could mean they would have to run back to their squad car and risk a heart attack. They were now shouting all manner of confusing instructions at Reggie, 'get out of the vehicle, lie down, kneel, show us your hands, walk backwards, throw the keys out the window.'

'I wish they'd make their minds up, I wonder what they want.'

Reggie was about to find out as he was pepper sprayed and dragged from his car, 'Spread 'em you thug, hands on the bonnet now, keep them out of your pockets. Do as you're told. Murph, keep an eye on his old lady.'

Murph waddled around the vehicle to the passenger side, noticing a bag of wraps on the backseat as he went. 'Okay lady, what's with the drugs then? Dealing are we?'

'Drugs? Oh, you mean those herbal things. We got them off a nice young man back at the last diner. He said they were good for headaches and Reggie, that's my husband over there collapsed on the bonnet, is blind as a bat since he lost his glasses yesterday and was having the most awful headaches. Terrible things headaches aren't they . . .' She would have continued but was helped forcefully out of the vehicle to join Reggie at the front.

Betty could see that Reggie was sniffling and snotty with the effects of pepper spray and reached into her handbag for a tissue. She didn't get far as she was instantly dropped by Murph's tazer. Amused at the peculiar way she had convulsed and collapsed in a crumpled heap, Murph hid a smile and said to his partner in justice, 'Okay, Buster, I got her covered, she was going for something in her bag. I'll cuff the old girl then radio in for a tow truck and the drug squad.'

It would all be on their dash camera as evidence, the dopey woman had reached for a weapon (allegedly) and for the safety of the honourable and public-spirited officer's protection she had to be neutralised. Murph rolled Betty over with his foot and clamped the Acme Mk8 restraint enforcers on her wrists as tight as they would go. 'Small wrists, Buster, small wrists. Watch him, watch him, he's coming around again.'

Not for long he wasn't, as Buster gave his tazer another outing. Reggie didn't mind, it dulled the pain of his arthritis and took his mind off trying to breathe.

They had a good view from the back seat of the police car as they entered town but only Betty could read the big welcome signs. One was for the Skunk Fanciers Society's annual best of breed show and the other was the annual dinner for democrat enthusiasts of The Wyoming State Psychiatric Clinic. She would have taken a photo but her camera had been confiscated. Later, some of her photos would star as exhibits for the prosecution, an honour that gave her mixed emotions.

On arrival at the police station the officers now had the problem of shifting their prisoners from car to cells and one of Reggie's Acme restraint enforcers had slipped off his wrist making him more dangerous. It took four plump, sorry burly, officers to remove the almost comatose arthritic pensioner from the vehicle. He was pinned to the ground by a twenty stone officer who repeatedly screamed at him to stop resisting . . . all caught on CCTV for evidence. 'You filthy limey drug mule stop resisting,' he screamed as he tried to wrench Reggie' arm behind his back. Even a rudimentary knowledge of anatomy or even his own personal experience should have clearly informed the officer that his prisoner's arm could never reach his back from that direction.

After all their recent suffering, a night in the cells proved quite relaxing and the bedding bench and en suite facilities were far better than at Hotel Cukaracha. It was also free.
After being seen by a doctor, photographed naked, finger printed and fed a breakfast of pancakes and coffee, all recorded for supporting evidence, the unhappy couple were ready to meet the judge, clear up all the misunderstanding and get on their way, they wouldn't even press charges of false arrest. All they wanted was to complete their holiday of a lifetime and on which they had invested their life savings to visit the land of the free and the home of the brave

The courthouse was only next door and by ten in the morning they were escorted in chains to their place of persecution – I mean, prosecution - Buster took the lead with Reggie limping along behind him, followed by Betty and Murph. As they began the climb the few steps to the place where the guilty stood, Reggie's arthritic right knee gave way and he fell forward, he reached out and grabbed whatever was in front of him. Reggie's flailing and desperate hands took as firm a grasp as they could on Buster's gun belt . . . Buster froze, stuck his hands in the air and pleaded for mercy. There was a bang, Buster wet himself and Reggie fell to the ground tazered. 'Got him, got the swine trying to disarm an officer,' yelled Murph, hoping if he said it loud enough some small reward or commendation might come his way. After a few moments of confusion and embarrassment they finally got Reggie into the dock where he stood dazed and slumped forward.

A squeaky angry voice screamed out, 'stand up straight man, stand up and look at me when I'm speaking, for god's sake you snivelling coward stand up!'

With the hand chains connected to the leg irons the only way Reggie could straighten his back was by bending his knees and he wasn't going to last long like that. He gave it a try though and looked up at a red-faced judge with traces of white powder under his nose and a pretty animal badge on his lapel. . . a small black and white animal with a bushy stand up tail!

'We'll teach you filthy foreign scum to bring drugs into our beloved country. The state will generously attempt to find someone willing to defend you if you cannot afford an attorney. I have other more important things to do today and then am on holiday for a month. The dopey looking woman is dismissed on bail of thirty dollars if she has that much, it looks like she hasn't a clue what she was doing but that wretched spaced out drug dealing animal is remanded for two months. That should be plenty of time to ensure a conviction by the state prosecution.'

'See you at dinner,' called Betty to Reggie as they were led away in different directions. She didn't, nor for supper either . . . even if they had one in Wyoming State Penitentiary.

There was only one lawyer in the state that was willing to take Reggie's case and he'd have done it for nothing if he had to. Bob Lincoln JD LLM was a rabid republican and had old scores to settle with that poison dwarf, recovering alcoholic specimen that dared call himself a judge. Yes, judge Arnie Benedict had once sentenced Bob's uncle to three months for organising a charity skunk hunt in aid of the Trump campaign. The judge however, was desperate to be seen to do well, he needed to prove himself a pillar of society and staunch defender of justice. Sending this foreign drug dealer down for a few years would go a long way to buy votes for the next municipal election of officers. It promised to be a challenging trial but a trial with only one true outcome.

The couple sold their lovely house in Kent with all its contents at a knock down price to Grabbit and Runn Estate agents London WW1. The dollar was highly buoyant against the pound and a few more thousand were lost in exchange rates and transfer fees but it was enough to keep Betty in a hostel and pay Mr Lincoln his fee.

Once the Judge was back from his subsidised holiday at the Nancy Pelosi Happy Park, California, the trial began. The judge dragged his feet at every turn, he wanted to capitalise on the press coverage for maximum effect.

The local rag, The Sundance Cryer, (Yes, that's how they spelled it) ran a daily update.

'Police Officer Murph in tears as he recalls the arrest. He sobbed, 'I just wanted to go home safe to my old lonely grandmother who I care for, but my brave colleague and I had to face down a vicious drug crazed maniac that tried first to run from us then resist arrest. I'm sorry, it's been too much for me.' The judge gave him the day off to recover from the trauma and the trial was adjourned for the day at ten past ten in the morning. New update tomorrow, 'Buster to spill the beans'.

After 3 months, Betty's travel visa ran out and she was deported … the good news being, deportation flights are free.

As their hire car was detained by the prosecution and the anti-democrat sticker used as an exhibit, the hire charges kept accruing and Reggie was charged with grand theft auto. The hire company are currently pursuing Betty's extradition from the UK.

Bob Lincoln was disbarred and spent the rest of his life in a secure psychiatric unit funded by the Democratic Party of USA where he was treated for a rare form of anti-establishment psychosis.

Murph and Buster were both promoted and awarded State Citations for Bravery above and beyond the call of duty.

Reggie was found not guilty of all drug related charges but found guilty of failing to obey a lawful order by an officer of the law, attempting to flee the scene, resisting arrest, assault on an officer in an attempt to take a lethal weapon, contempt of court for not standing straight when the judge passed sentence, (he'd actually fainted from shock).

Reggie was given 5 years in the state penitentiary. He settled in well, treating his arthritis with homemade drugs manufactured in the prison kitchen and landing a plum job in the prison library teaching the inmates English as a Foreign Language. He proved very popular with the prisoners who all seemed to be ex gun club republican supporters and skunk haters.

The UK Foreign Office stated that all that could be done was being done to bring Reggie home to his loving wife Betty, who was living in a one bedroomed flat on social handouts in a rough suburb of Wolverhampton.

Reggie was better off in the land of the free and the home of the brave … Wyoming State Penitentiary.

The Funeral Note

He'd not seen his good friend for many years and now he was going to see her for one last time - at rest in her coffin. He was truly sorry, for this was a great loss to him and he felt an enduring curse that he hadn't made more of an effort before.

Her husband wasn't a religious man, but he was a good man, yes indeed, and he'd faithfully followed his wife's wishes to the letter for her final journey. The flowers to buy, the guests to invite, the clothes she chose, the music and poems, even the menu for the wake was preordained. Even that she wished the coffin should remain open as she lay at rest in the dining room of their little house so that her spirit self could say goodbye to each soul who visited.

'Go on through, take as long as you like, she's not going anywhere,' said her husband, 'I'll put the kettle on again – that'll be dead next – with all the use it's getting.'

Thanking him and with a nod of respect, he turned and entered the room. It was odd; she didn't look any different from normal except he wasn't on the end of the cheeky abuse she often saved just for him. He stood a while, quietly offering his wishes for a peaceful after-life while distantly hearing the clatter of cups and saucers from the kitchen. As he looked down, he noticed a small roll of paper enclosed in her right hand. He was alone, curiosity gained the better of him and he gently lifted the paper, unrolled it and began to read. . .

There's something that I want to say
but now, you'll never know.
I'll leave it to another day,
To say, 'I love you so.'

Why not say, these things before?
It's all to do with me,
while you were distant, on far shore,
it's me, you could not see.

There was more, but just then, her husband called from the kitchen, 'tea's done mate, and biscuits, she even told me what sort to buy. Don't want crumbs in the coffin, come on through and meet the neighbours in the garden.'

He panicked, he knew he should not have read the note, it was private, how could he have been so thoughtless. Embarrassed, he struggled with shaking hands to put it back but as though to stop him, her hand was now closed tight.

Just as the door opened to the shout of, 'tea's getting cold mate,' he quickly shoved the note into his jacket pocket. Let's face it, no one would ever notice, no one would ever know.

Some years later, it was his own time to take the last drive in a posh car. The lid was screwed down and all was ready. 'Oh,' said the undertaker to the man's son, 'there was this note he wanted to take with him, but my assistant has closed the lid now. Did you want me to reopen the casket?'

'No, give it here and I'll chuck it in the bin. Knowing him it's just some old mumbo jumbo, he was always writing weird and meaningless stuff. I never had time to read any of it mind you. Well, let's get this over with; I've got lots of important things to do.'

With a touch his usual good fortune there was a suitable bin in the kitchen, and crumpled, in it went, never to be read again.

Shap to Ingelby Cross – a walk in the park.

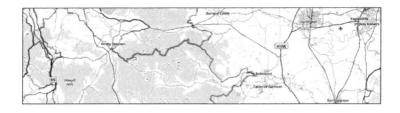

It was to be a 4-day expedition from Shap to Ingelby Cross in August 1993. There were three days of rain, solid rain, and one day of no rain in which all the flies who had been hiding from the rain came out hungry.

At 0815 hours in horizontal rain I started walking east, fortified by a huge breakfast. After about seven miles I met some other walkers who told me that the route had changed from that shown in my old book, (bit of a blow that, but the book was at least 16 years old). Their information did not become part of my navigational knowledge sadly and I ended up being threatened by a cow and lost to boot. You might think this funny but cows can be very aggressive, let's face it some stranger is walking dirty boots all over their dinner, wouldn't you be a little tetchy? At nine miles I sat by Sunbiggin Tarn, took off my wet boots and socks, had my packed lunch and was asked by the ten little piggies to take their photo. At thirteen miles I stopped at a great B&B called Bents Farm. I enjoyed tea and scones in the lounge and read some sheep farmer's cartoon books. Hilarious they were too, mostly about sheep and their seeming death wish from the moment they are born. One cartoon depicted an auction ring with a farmer desperately giving mouth to mouth to a sheep. The auctioneer said, "I'm very sorry farmer Bloggs but I really think you're going to have to accept that it's dead!"

At 0900 hours next day I left Bents Farm – in the rain-within 200 yards my feet were wet again. Following the book's guidance, at about seven miles on I climbed over a wall and promptly landed over the tops of my boots in slurry. At Kirkby Stephen I bought some apple pies and gave my postcards to a passing postman. At fourteen miles into the day I'd climbed the mind sapping utter slog to Nine Standards Rig, everywhere was bog, bog and more bog. I put on dry socks, after the ten piggies had a photo shoot, and I ate those apple pies. I'd made pencil notes in the book on the mapped section and on page 79 it reads, '15 miles, bog, bog. 16 miles bog, 17 miles bog, bog, 18 miles bog, bog, at 19 miles the stream I was supposed to cross was so swollen by the continual rain that it was too high for any safe crossing. At just about 20 miles I stopped at a B&B. It was a strange place but had a few other guests too. I had a very welcome warm bath – a much nicer type of water than I had encountered all day I think. The water was brown- as it came out of the tap, probably straight off the fells.

The next day my note in the book shows a tea shop, closed, at nine miles on in Reeth, and just after that the first mention of flies. This, then, must be the day of the flies, and, no rain. At 18 miles it reads, 'flies and thirsty, 19 miles, flies, 20 miles flies, 21 miles flies. It took 10 agonising hours to get here from the other side of Keld. Found B&B, had bath, found a pub for dinner then home to a summerhouse to try and sleep'. The ten little piggies rested in the summer house– which was the only available accommodation I could find, the bath was in the house, the bed in the garden.) It rained all night. I later discovered that this was the wettest August day on record in Yorkshire.

Leaving the town of Richmond, at about 4 miles along

my way, I lost it. Luckily some people on horseback came by. I questioned them and they kindly gave me some advice on the route. I took their advice and within two to three hundred yards I was floundering on steep mud slopes through low bush like trees, probably Hawthorn, and my route cut off by raging torrents. My blistered and again soaked feet I had to kick into the muddy slopes to obtain footholds and my fingers likewise had to be driven in to help my climb out. When I finally fought my way out of this predicament, the blessed relief was short lived when I found myself on the same track as those creatures on horseback and only a short way from where I'd spoken to them. I only hope they heard me!

At 11 miles I met people who told me that I could have got to this point by a new route, however it transpired that it would have been no quicker. (A prerequisite for engaging in any new route I would say, especially at this juncture in the walk). At 14 miles into the day I signed the visitor's book at Danby Wiske Pub. By now I had noticed something interesting; there was less pain while continuously walking, as I remember. Any stop, like to sign the book, meant some considerable pain when starting to move the feet again. I sang a few songs, thought a lot – mostly about lying in the grass verge and dying. At 18 miles I scrawled, 'exhausted' in the book, and two miles later find a sign that explains how the path has been conveniently (for them that is!) lengthened by farmers so that you don't walk by their farmhouse. Just what the knackered walker needs I'd say. At 1815 hours after 9 hours rain walking the 23 miles of the day and my journey were over. Thank God for that.

It's the pain of that journey that long after makes me smile.

Goodbyes.

When someone leaves, they take a part of us with them.
It is this which calls to us from afar in the sorrows of loss.
We await its return in hope but sometimes it never does.

***

Thank you for reading my stories, Richard.

The mirror has no eyes that see and the Heron looks beyond.
Reflection must obey the Heron's every move.
Meanwhile, the fish travels to a destiny of its own making and
reflected in a different world . The mirror keeps its secret.

It's so much
fun, raking
these from
puddles

Only the deer, the rabbit and me. . .

Printed in Great Britain
by Amazon

77535025R00123